MY SECRET GRIEF

ON THE OUTSIDE LOOKING IN

Jayme Lynn

My Secret Grief © 2021 by Jayme Lynn. All rights reserved.

Published by Author Academy Elite
PO Box 43, Powell, OH 43065
www.AuthorAcademyElite.com

All rights reserved. This book contains material protected under International and Federal Copyright Laws and Treaties. Any unauthorized reprint or use of this material is prohibited. No part of this book may be reproduced or transmitted in any form or by any means, electronic or mechanical, including photocopying, recording, or by any information storage and retrieval system, without express written permission from the author.

Identifiers:
LCCN: 2021902178
ISBN: 978-1-64746-711-1 (paperback)
ISBN: 978-1-64746-712-8 (hardback)
ISBN: 978-1-64746-713-5 (ebook)

Available in paperback, hardback, and e-book

Any Internet addresses (websites, blogs, etc.) and telephone numbers printed in this book are offered as a resource. They are not intended in any way to be or imply an endorsement by Author Academy Elite, nor does Author Academy Elite vouch for the content of these sites and numbers for the life of this book.

Some names and identifying details have been changed to protect the privacy of individuals.

Dedication:

To my husband and best friend Roger, you've made me laugh and wiped away my tears. Although our life together didn't turn as we planned, our infertility journey made us stronger together. I love you!

To my father, who always told me, you'll never be wrong if you write from the heart.

Contents

Prologue vii
Chapter 1 1
Chapter 2 6
Chapter 3 17
Chapter 4 25
Chapter 5 33
Chapter 6 38
Chapter 7 47
Chapter 8 62
Chapter 9 72
Chapter 10 81
Chapter 11 85
Chapter 12 90
Chapter 13 98
Chapter 14 110
Chapter 15 114
Chapter 16 122
Chapter 17 133
Chapter 18 136
Chapter 19 147
Chapter 20 159
About the Author 171

Prologue

The dirt crumbled beneath my fingers as I tried to climb out of the hole. I fell back down onto my butt and looked up. I could still see daylight -- to my relief, I wasn't too far down in the darkness. No one knows I'm here - how the hell am I going to get out of here? I thought to myself. I could feel my anxiety creeping in, my heart racing, my breathing quicken, and beads of sweat forming on my face.

It was dark in the hole. I wiped the sweat from my forehead and could feel the dampness of my curly hair that rested on my neck- *Gross*. I sat there, contemplating my next move. Okay, let's try this again, Jess. I dug my hands into the dirt, planted my foot into the wall, and tried to hoist myself up. *Who are you kidding, fatso? What makes you think you can pull yourself out of here?* I jabbed the dirt wall with my clenched fists several times until they ached, and I started rubbing them. I let out an agonizing, desperate, frustrated scream before I slumped down to the ground and began to sob. I started twirling my hair to calm myself down and think.

The deafening silence frightened me, and I twirled my hair more and more. When I finally stopped, I started stroking my hair at the top of my head with my thumb and index finger, section by section, until I found a thick, coarse piece of hair and plucked it from my head. I touched the root bulb to my lips; it felt wet, sticky, and satisfying; a little bit of calmness crept in.

PROLOGUE

    Although I couldn't see the hair in the darkness I was in, I bit off the bulb with my teeth and then proceeded to take tiny bites of the hair until it was gone, and I swallowed it. I then searched for my next piece of hair to satisfy my uncontrollable urge, and then another and another until my mania was satisfied. I thought I had put this ritual behind me. Long gone were the days of sitting in my closet fort after school, pulling out my hair to calm myself after being tormented all day by my bully, Kimmy. My trichotillomania was resurfacing, and I couldn't stop it. How far would I go?

    Thoughts and questions started racing through my head again. What about Vinny and mom? They don't know I'm here. Are they even looking for me? How long have I been down here? I started to panic again; this time, I had my fingers in my mouth, my tongue tracing along the already jagged edge of my fingernail. I rubbed the end of my nail along the end of my teeth, trying to smooth it out. I bit off the dry skin along the sides of my nails and spit it out on the ground, then moving to the nail itself. I bit my fingernails down to nubs, painfully short and slightly bleeding. I worked so hard to grow my nails, and within a few minutes, my fingers were once again stubby, squared, and unfeminine. My chest was heaving, and I felt my heart beating fast and heard its echo in my ears. I stood up with tears streaming down my face. I started to yell. Help! Help! Can anyone hear me? Please, someone, help me! I'm down here. Please, anyone? My voice trembled. Can you hear me? I said in a weak, almost whisper tone. I sank to the ground in the fetal position, sobbing into the crook of my arm.

    I sat up and wiped the tears from my face. Breathe Jessica. I took a deep, slow breath in through my nose while counting to five. One. Two. Three. Four. Five. I held it for a count of two. One. Two. Then I released the breath slowly through my mouth for a count of five. One. Two. Three. Four. Five. I repeated the process several more times. My heartbeat regulated, and

MY SECRET GRIEF

I wiped the last of my tears from my cheeks. I was feeling more focused, calm, and in control, and the anxiety subsided. I learned this technique in my psychiatrist's office and used it often. Now in a more relaxed mindset, I recalled the events of the day.

I had driven from Lily Lake, the rural area where I live, to Chicago's Western Suburbs, where I had grown up, about an hour and a half drive. I planned a surprise party for my brother Jason's 50th birthday with help from my mom, half-sister Mindi, and Jason's wife, Amber. He is a big fan of the Peanuts Gang, so it was only fitting we have a Peanut's/Charlie Brown-themed party. "Good Grief Jason's 50," the invitations read. We are Irish Twins, siblings born in the same year.

Today, Jason's 50th surprise birthday party went off as planned. We had it at our favorite restaurant, the Dog House. Even though they were famous for their hot dogs and beef sandwiches, their pizza was outstanding. I missed good Chicago Style Pizza since moving out to the country. This pizza had the most fantastic buttery, flaky crust, and they were generous with the toppings; mushrooms and pepperoni were my two favorites. The weather was beautiful for this mid-May day, not too hot with a gentle breeze blowing.

I asked to move the party outside onto the patio. I set up a gift and dessert table with my homemade decorated dark chocolate cupcakes topped with yellow frosting. I adorned the tables with yellow and black streamers and a Happy 50th Birthday sign.

I made little box favors that looked like Charlie Brown's yellow t-shirt with black zig-zag stripe three-quarters of the way down to the bottom of the t-shirt. I filled them with candy, one for each guest, and placed them in front of everyone's plate. I made two for Jason, one filled with candy rocks so he could quote Charlie Brown himself and say, "I got a rock" I knew that would make him chuckle. The other t-shirt box favor, just

PROLOGUE

like everyone else's, was filled with nostalgic candies from our childhood. Including Zots, candy buttons, Bazooka Bubble Gum, Wacky Wafers, Sixlets, BB Bats, Razzles, Chicklets, and liquid-filled wax bottles, just to name a few.

My half-sister, Mindi, of course, had her input. Mindi said I should have bought a cake and had it professionally decorated because my cupcakes are always dry, and they don't look professional. Complete bullshit. Friends and family love my desserts and how cute I make everything look. But once again, I let her into my head. I blew it off and said, well, I was trying to save money. Mindi is four years older than me and not the older sister I had wanted. She always belittled me and picked on me, making me feel bad about myself and my talents. The worst thing was when we were young; she did it behind my mom and dad's back, so she never got caught. She would whisper words in my ear like, why are you so fat? Or did you shower today? Because you stink. She did this every chance she got since I was about age seven or eight, maybe even before, I can't remember. I never said anything to my parents because she threatened to physically hurt me if I did, rearrange my pretty face as she put it. "Remember, snitches, get stitches." Followed by a pinch on my upper arm that left a bruise, which was always covered by my sleeve. I think she was jealous because she didn't have an ounce of creativity, and being creative was my happy place, or maybe she just liked being mean.

I longed for the simpler days when we were kids, not having a care in the world outside playing with friends, the few I had, and just having a good time. We played tag, hide-and-seek, red light – green light, and mother, may I? These were some of my favorites. We explored our neighborhood both on foot and on our bikes. We went down to the pond to catch tadpoles or frogs, skip rocks and look for fossils and arrowheads. Sometimes I wished I could go back to the way things were, and sometimes I'm glad to be out of the growing pains.

Jason was enjoying the party; it was nice to have family and old friends together. He, indeed, was surprised. As he walked up to the restaurant, he saw his best friend, Tim, sitting at the patio table. At first, he didn't put two and two together; he just thought it was a happy coincidence that Tim was there. As he looked around, he saw all of us, and we yelled surprise! I was kind of surprised that my mom didn't let the cat out of the bag as she has a habit of sometimes doing.

The pizza was fantastic but spending time with friends and family was better. I missed my family more than I thought I would when we moved for Vinny's job. Even though the drive was only an hour and a half away, it just wasn't the same not having my family less than twenty minutes away, my mom's rule - no one could live more than twenty minutes away from someone else. My mom enjoyed having her children and grandchildren close. If they needed her or she needed them, everyone was close enough to help each other out or simply get together for an impromptu dinner or game night. I broke the rule and tried to visit as much as possible.

We had fun reminiscing and remembering old stories of our childhood "adventures" with our friends. I grabbed a seat next to Tim, Jason's best friend since the age of five.

"Hi, Tim! How have you been?"

"Hi, Jessica!" "I've been well, busy with work; you know the usual. The kids are almost all grown up, my oldest boy is heading off to college this fall, and my youngest boy will be a senior in high school." He pulled out pictures from his wallet to show me.

"Handsome, young men," I replied. "They look just like you!" "I remember you and Jason played baseball every day in the summer from sun up to sundown. Do your boys play any sports?"

"Yeah, they are both into hockey and are quite good."

"Tim, do you remember when we flooded the field next to our house and skated on it in the winter?"

PROLOGUE

"Yeah, that was fun! Remember the giant hill we used to sled down?"

"We had some great adventures!"

I excused myself to mingle and check to see if anyone needed anything.

I was sure to take plenty of pictures to scrapbook later and make Jason a copy as well. It was kind of weird to be sitting there with childhood friends who all had kids of their own now, most of whom were getting ready to go off to college. Some of our friends were even becoming grandparents! Where had the time gone? I felt like I blinked and poof; I'm almost 50 myself! My thoughts wandered back to the same questions I've been asking for years and years; why hadn't God blessed me with a family? I felt the all-familiar sensation of not being a mom well up inside of me. I excused myself to go to the restroom to collect myself, so I didn't have a complete meltdown during Jason's birthday party; I could do that when I got home.

The party was coming to an end. We were saying our good-byes, promising our friends not to let too much time pass before we saw each other again. Jason, who is usually reserved, was talkative and genuinely happy that his friends and family came out to celebrate him. My mission was complete, another successful, enjoyable party in the books. More importantly, I managed to get through a party without having a complete meltdown of my non-mom status.

I left for my hour and a half ride home back to the country and stopped for gas. When I got back on the road, I managed to get myself turned around and took a wrong turn. There were a lot of newly constructed homes. Land that was once vacant was now thriving with new subdivisions and unrecognizable. I drove around for forty-five minutes, nothing looked familiar, and it scared me. I finally found my way to the road I should have been on in the first place. I started my trek home. I wanted to get back before it became dark, I had a hard time seeing in the dark, and the pups still needed to be fed. I put my favorite Bruce Springsteen CD in the CD player and turned up the volume as the road home is relatively dull. The land is flat in the Midwest, just one farm after another, occasionally seeing some cows, sheep, horses, cornfields, and wind turbines.

* * *

As I sat staring in the darkness, I knew I had a choice to make. Remain here in the hole, sad, depressed, and unfulfilled, letting grief devour me or stand up, put on my big girl pants, and face my demons. Either road would not be easy and have its own set of obstacles. Would I take anyone on this journey with me? Would it lead to my demise, or would it lead me to victory?

PROLOGUE

Jessica's Dark Chocolate Cake

Anyone can pick up a boxed cake mix and bake a cake. Boxed cake mixes have come a long way, but for me, nothing replaces a cake made from scratch because you can't package love, and love is the ingredient that makes a recipe special. "I made this cake from scratch for you because I love you."

Jessica Fontana

Ingredients:

2 cups of sugar
1-3/4 cups all-purpose flour
3/4 cup dark cocoa powder
1-1/2 teaspoon baking powder
1-1/2 teaspoon baking soda
1 teaspoon salt
2 eggs
1 cup whole milk
2 teaspoons pure vanilla extract
1/2 cup vegetable oil
1/4 cup hot black coffee (optional)*
3/4 cup boiling water (if not using coffee, increase boiling water to 1 cup)*

Directions:

Pre-heat oven to 350 degrees. Spray 9 x 13 pan with Pam cooking spray (bottom and all sides). This can also be made in a greased and floured Bundt pan – bake 45 minutes or in two greased and floured 9-inch round baking pans – bake 30 to 35 minutes.

Stir together sugar, flour, cocoa, baking powder, baking soda, and salt in a large bowl. Add eggs, milk, oil, and vanilla. Beat with an electric mixer on medium speed for 2 minutes. *Stir in hot coffee and boiling water mix well – batter will be very thin and water-like. Pour into a prepared pan. Bake for 35 to 40 minutes until a knife inserted comes out clean. Cool completely and frost with Dark Chocolate Frosting (see below). Makes 10-12 servings.

Dark Chocolate Frosting

Ingredients:

1 stick salted butter
2/3 cup dark cocoa powder
3 cups powdered sugar
1/3 cup whole milk
1 teaspoon vanilla extract

Directions:

Melt butter and stir in cocoa. Alternately add powdered sugar and milk, beating to spreading consistency. May add a small amount of additional milk if needed. Stir in vanilla. Frost the cake.

Enjoy! Jessica

Chapter 1

As I laid in a stranger's bed, a weird feeling flushed through my body and made me shiver internally. I only felt that feeling one other time in my life at the age of ten. I was riding my bike on the sidewalk, a motorcycle zipping up and down the street. I thought to myself, I hope he doesn't get into an accident. I felt a shiver flow through my body. A few moments later, the guy lost control of the motorcycle, jumped the curb, hit the front tire of my bicycle, sending me flying through the air and into a clump of bushes. The guy jumped off, and the motorcycle came to a crashing halt as it hit a car parked in the garage. I walked away with a few bruises, and the guy was taken away in an ambulance.

I shook off the shiver and headed to the bathroom to use the toilet, brush my teeth and hair. I quietly walked back into the room, trying not to wake my friend Kelly who was somewhere under a mound of blue blankets. I opened the shades to let in some sunlight and warmth into the room. I straightened her roommate's bed that I had slept in the night before.

"Kell? You up?" Inaudible mumbling erupted from under the mound of blue blankets. "Do you have any food? I'm starving." Kelly's arm emerged from under the blankets and pointed to the mini-fridge.

"Yogurt," she mumbled. She slowly climbed out of the blanket, sat at the edge of her bed, squinting, still dressed in the clothes she had worn to the frat party the night before, her hair looking like she had stuck her finger in an electrical

CHAPTER 1

outlet. "Aspirin," she said in a gravelly voice. I grabbed two aspirin and a bottle of water and handed them to her. We sat in silence as I finished my yogurt. She was in no condition to spend the day together. I closed the blinds and tucked her into bed.

"I'm going to head home. Thank you for inviting me to the party. I had a good time." I lied. I had hoped to meet someone, and I hadn't. "I'll let you sleep it off. Call me later."

"Okay, bye Jess."

"Bye."

I drove the forty-five minutes from the college back to my subdivision. When I pulled into my neighborhood, I felt the inkling once again; something was wrong. I saw my Uncle Bill's car as I pulled into the driveway. I parked the car, grabbed my overnight bag, and rushed inside. Mom, Dad, and Uncle Bill were sitting at the dining room table, talking and crying. My brother Jason, half-sister Mindi, and two cousins, Greg and Paul, were seated in the family room in silence, tears flowing down their faces.

"What happened?" I said, panicked. My mom got up from the table, walked over to me, and hugged me.

"Gram had another heart attack this morning. She didn't make it."

"Oh, no." My lip quivered as tears filled my eyes. "I'm sorry, mom." I held her close to me. I then walked over and slumped into the only available spot on the couch with my siblings and cousins. Jason handed me the box of tissues. We sat in almost complete silence; the only sound accompanying our empty stares was our whimpering, sniffling, and blowing our noses.

"I remember playing cards with Gram ever since I was little." "We played Go-Fish, war, and rummy." "She enjoyed playing cards," Greg said.

We nodded and shared other memories.

As I sat on the couch clutching a pillow to my abdomen, dabbing tears away with a tissue, beautiful memories of my Gram came to mind. My earliest memories were of me outside in my playpen, watching Gram put the laundry on the clothesline to dry. When I was a toddler, she played with me in my pretend kitchen when I cooked or had tea parties for my dolls and stuffed animals. When I was a little older, I remember coming home from school, and I went straight to see her. We sat and ate graham crackers, dunked in milk or saltine crackers and butter, and talked about my day. I loved spending time in the kitchen with her too. She taught me how to cook, and I often helped her in the kitchen on Sundays when we gathered for our big family meal. I started baking with her at the age of six. We made cookies for my dad, as he loved sweets, and those are my favorite memories. I still use the rolling pin my grandpa carved for her.

Gram was a master of crochet and knitting. She tried to teach me, but I couldn't get the hang of it. She told stories of coming to America as a teenager from Czechoslovakia. She helped her family run a grocery store and helped her aunt, uncle, and cousins with their tailor shop. We often talked about how she met grandpa, a home builder who built many of the Bungalows in Chicago and Berwyn. I think she will be remembered the most for all the good Bohemian food and desserts she made for us. I loved her stuffing, coffee cakes, Kolacky cookies, listy and apple strudel, I remembered, licking my lips.

I thought about how incredibly strong she was. She was a widow early, survived a couple of heart attacks, and was a double-leg amputee due to diabetes. That didn't stop her. She learned how to use her artificial legs. She baked and cooked for us and helped mom with the chores she was able to do. I never heard her complain, not once.

CHAPTER 1

The funeral was intimate, just immediate family; her children, grandchildren, a sister, and a couple of nieces and nephews. She didn't have any living friends.

I walked up to the casket to say my final good-bye. Gram wore a black dress; her snow-white hair pulled back into a bun. She had on a little face powder, blush, lipstick, and eyeglasses. The bottom of the casket was closed as she didn't have any legs. "Good-bye, Gram. I'm going to miss baking with you, playing cards, and our talks. I love you." I managed to whisper to her through my tears. I took my seat next to Jason and continued to cry through the remainder of the service.

After the funeral service, we gathered at a Bohemian restaurant for lunch and celebrated my Gram's life, talking, laughing, and sharing fond memories and stories of her. When we arrived home, it was strange walking into the house. My Gram, who had lived with us our entire lives, was no longer there. The house didn't smell of something delicious cooking or baking. Those comforting aromas reminded me I was home. As I hung up my coat in the closet, my Gram's artificial legs and walker were inside, stressing the permanence of the day's events. Gram's passing left a hole in my heart that day.

MY SECRET GRIEF

Kolacky Cookie

Ingredients:

1 cup butter
1 8oz package cream cheese
1 tablespoon sugar
1 tablespoon whole milk
1 egg yolk, beaten
1 1/2 cups flour
1/2 teaspoon baking powder
1 can Solo brand filling (any flavor)

Directions:

Pre-heat oven to 400 degrees.

Cream together the butter, cream cheese, milk, and sugar. Add beaten egg yolk. Sift together flour and baking powder. Add to cream cheese mixture and blend well. Refrigerate 4 hours or overnight.

Roll or pat out on a well-floured board to 1/4 inch thickness and cut with a round cookie cutter or juice glass 2 inches around. Place on an ungreased cookie sheet. Make a depression with your thumb or spoon in the center of each round. Fill centers with a scant teaspoon of Solo filling.

Bake 400 degrees for 10 to 15 minutes or until lightly browned. Sprinkle with confectioners' sugar before serving. Makes approximately 36 cookies.

Enjoy! Jessica

Chapter 2

Adam was a boy who lived down the street. Our parents attended high school together and have remained friends. Adam is a few years older than me and is better friends with Jason and Mindi. My mom had mentioned to his mom that I was looking for a summer job, and, with his help, I got my first job at the Dog House, a trendy restaurant and bar where Adam worked.

Lorenzo, the Dog House owner, didn't hire just anyone, you had to know someone to work there, and I knew Adam. Adam quit the Dog House to attend college shortly after I started. I enjoyed working there. It was an extended family. Everyone worked together as a team, and it was enjoyable and not like work at all. I had friends of all ages from age eighteen up into the sixties. Lorenzo had trained us on his specific method of efficiency, and the atmosphere was positive. We hung out after work; some dated each other, and some have met their spouses at the Dog House and have gotten married and started families of their own. Working there was a good distraction when life sometimes wasn't going too well.

I started at the Dog House like most of the wait staff, bussing tables, washing dishes, sweeping and mopping the floor, cleaning the bathrooms, and emptying the trash. After three months, I graduated to the counter, taking orders and running the cash register. I had always been shy, but I was coming out of my shell since working at the Dog House.

Betty's brownies were the best I'd ever tasted; she has a secret recipe that she would never share. What I wanted most was to help Betty with the baking. I needed to muster up the courage to ask her. It would be another month before I did just that.

"Betty? May I talk to you about something?"

"Sure, dear, what's on your mind?"

"Betty, I wanted to know if you needed any help with the baking. I baked with my Gram all the time since the age of six, to be exact. I think I'm pretty good at it, and I would love to help you out."

"Well, I have enough help right now, and we need you on the counter, taking orders and running the register. If one of the girls who is helping me right now leaves, I will let you know."

I withheld a sigh and tried to hide my disappointment. "Okay, thanks," I said.

I continued as counter help. I still enjoyed it and the customers. I helped with packaging the desserts hoping that would keep me on Betty's radar. It was the end of summer, and one of Betty's bakers was leaving to get married.

"Jessica, one of the girls in the bakery, is leaving. I would like you to join me in the bakery kitchen when needed. We need you to continue working the counter, taking orders, and running the cash register. What do you think?"

I could barely conceal my delight and smiled, "of course, I would love that!" Working with Betty in the kitchen brought back fond memories of my Gram. With the aroma of chocolate in the air, it felt like home. We made huge batches of brownies and cut and packaged them up daily. They rarely lasted past noon. Soon Betty added chocolate cake and cookies— chocolate chip, sugar, and peanut butter. The Dog House sold out of baked goods every single day.

Lorenzo expanded once again and added an ice cream parlor. He bought vanilla, chocolate, and strawberry ice cream from a vendor with an over 100-year-old recipe. It indeed

CHAPTER 2

was the best ice cream I had ever tasted, and I'm not a big ice cream person. I continued to help Betty bake in the morning and make ice cream sundaes in the afternoon. Betty trained me on how to make all the old-fashioned ice cream creations. I had never thought much about it, but there was some artistry needed to build these creations. We used the traditional glass ice cream dishes and decorated the inside with the sauce—chocolate, strawberry, caramel, or pineapple. The ice cream was the foundation, building off that with fruit, usually bananas or strawberries, more ice cream, and then the whipped cream topped with more sauce, nuts or sprinkles, a cherry on the top, and a sugar wafer on the side.

I was happy for the first time since losing my Gram. I loved making these ice cream creations and watching people's faces covered with waves of pleasure as they first tasted it with their eyes and then dove in with a spoon. Lorenzo's first year adding the ice cream parlor, he won an award for the Best Ice Cream Place in Chicago. The local paper wrote an article about the Dog House, and Lorenzo received a plaque to hang on the wall. He won many, many more times after that. I even got my picture in the newspaper showing off one of the ice cream creations, called the giant; I had just made it for a family; the picture hangs on the Dog House wall to this day. I couldn't wait to be a mom and bring my children here someday for an ice cream treat. My parents took us out for ice cream or a special treat when we received good grades in school or had something to celebrate. I wanted to keep this tradition with my children.

Summer ended, and my freshman year of community college was beginning, although I had not decided on a major. I knew I wanted to go into healthcare but not quite sure what field. I signed up for general classes and a medical terminology class, which was enjoyable; I found it engaging, and it was interesting to me. There were some pretty cute guys at community college, and I was still somewhat shy around the boys, always on the lookout for a boyfriend. Memories of my first high school dance emerged. My classmate Brian asked me to a high school dance, the closest I had come to dating in high school. We had arranged to meet at the dance, much to my disappointment, I was not the only girl he invited to the dance, and I left in tears. I guarded myself when it came to boys and dating. I attended college part-time and worked at the Dog House in the evening and on weekends, as usual. I lived at home with my parents and Jason.

In early fall, Mindi, the head cheerleader, married her high school sweetheart, Jeff, the high school quarterback, and moved out of the house. I no longer had to endure her bullying, and it was freeing. I was jealous of her, though. That's the dream I had - to marry my high school sweetheart. I could not wait to find the love of my life. I had it all planned out. My high school sweetheart and I would marry, and together, we would have six children, three boys, and three girls. We would design our home and have it built just the way we wanted, as my parents had done. A big backyard for the kids to play in, with a swing set and treehouse. Our house would be the one where all the neighborhood kids wanted to hang out. I would make fresh-baked cookies for them and serve milk or Kool-Aid. I wanted to hear the children laughing and having fun; it's one of my favorite sounds. The big snafu, however, I never had a high school sweetheart.

I had the day off from work, and my car was in the shop, so I asked my dad if he would drive me to the Dog House to pick up my paycheck. He obliged, and we sat and had lunch. My dad had a bacon cheeseburger, perhaps not the best choice after surviving a quadruple bypass just over a year ago, but my mom wasn't there, and she wouldn't know. I had a Maxwell Street polish sausage – a fried polish sausage topped with mustard and grilled onions. We sat and talked about nothing in particular.

CHAPTER 2

"How's college going? I know you just started, but how do you like it so far?" my dad asked.

"It's okay." "The school is pretty big, and I got lost once but managed to find my way to my class without being late. I like my teachers so far. I like my biology class and medical terminology class; they are my favorites. I do not like algebra; you know I'm not good at math like Jason."

"I'm sure Jason will help you out if you need it."

"I know, he's good like that."

"What about friends? Have you made any new friends?" he said, concerned.

"No, not yet. There is a new boy at work who is pretty cute; his name is Charlie. He works on the weekends, mostly because he is still in high school. He seems nice. I haven't talked to him yet, but when we work together next, Lorenzo asked me to help train him and show him the ropes." I found it easy to talk to my dad, we had similar personalities, and we always celebrated our birthdays together as they were two days apart. My dad always told me I was his favorite birthday gift.

"Just talk to him, be his friend, and then you will know if you have anything in common. You'll know if you want to date him or not."

"Okay, I'll try that. Thanks, dad."

My dad seemed different. I couldn't explain it, but I felt something was wrong. He seemed distracted and frigidity. He wasn't making a lot of eye contact when we talked and seemed nervous. I didn't know if I should ask or not. I decided not to ask. We weren't the kind of a family that shared everything, and it probably wasn't any of my business. I figured it was something to do with his job as finances had been very tight since his heart surgery, still paying off the doctor and hospital bills.

We walked to the car and started the drive home. We came to a stoplight, and my dad turned to me and said, "I have the big C."

I looked at him, surprised, "cancer?" I asked. *Cancer? Cancer is never a good thing.*

"Yes. I haven't told mom yet, and I don't know how to tell her," his voice cracked a little bit. "It will crush her."

"What kind?" I asked.

"Inoperable small cell lung cancer." "I'm going to have chemo and radiation treatments, and hopefully, that will take care of it."

I was shocked by the news, unsure what to say, and surprised he told me first. When I thought about it for a few minutes, it made sense. My dad had been a smoker since junior high school and only quite a couple of years ago after suffering a heart attack and subsequent heart surgery. "Dad, you have to tell mom, especially since you've already been to see the doctor by yourself. She should have been included and not kept in the dark. I'm sure she would have had a bazillion questions."

"I'll tell her when we get home. She will have to start taking me to my treatments anyway. She can ask all her questions then."

I think my dad was still in disbelief. He loved my mother very much, and they acted like lovey-dovey teenagers most of the time. I think he didn't know how to tell her, he didn't want to hurt her, and that's why he kept it from her.

He told her that night after dinner in their bedroom. I know because I could hear her crying as they talked. I'm sure she was scared, still relatively young, 48, to contemplate being a widow.

The next week we went to my dad's first round of chemo as a family. We were able to ask the doctor questions after he explained the treatment to us, as he had done with my father at his first appointment. I remember the doctor telling us it will be like we are on a roller coaster; there will be good days and bad days. He added, "The prognosis is two to five years."

CHAPTER 2

My dad's treatments started. I had never seen him look so unhealthy in my life, except for when he had a heart attack. He was pale, and he lost a lot of weight. He was a reasonably tall man, and now he was bony. His hair was coming out in clumps, one day, he shaved it all off. I was kind of afraid of him, and he didn't look like himself. I didn't know what to say, afraid to say the wrong thing, so I didn't say anything. I had a hard time even looking at him. I hated the way he looked. My strong, healthy, playful, funny dad was different; he was frail, and he slept a lot. He didn't join us at the dinner table most of the time because he lacked an appetite or was sick in the bathroom. There were no more game nights; he didn't have the stamina. I was in denial and spent a lot of time in my bedroom.

I spent a lot of time asking God not to take him, even though I had never been to church. Our family members who attended church seemed confident that God would answer their prayers when they were in need. They often said, "It's in God's hands," and seemed to be perfectly content that God would take care of the situation. I was desperate for my father to beat this.

My dad went through his treatments. He slept a lot, he barely ate, but he never complained, not once. After his treatment ended, my dad was in remission. He started putting on some weight, and his hair grew back thick, dark and curly, which was a bit shocking because it had once been fine, relatively straight, and light brown. Life was getting back to normal.

My dad only stayed in remission for a few months before his cancer came back, this time in his brain. This was the roller coaster ride the doctor had mentioned. Once again, he started treatment, lost his hair, and lost any weight he had gained. This time, though, he seemed more tired. He slept almost all day couldn't do much else. He appeared to be suffering more this time around from the side effects of chemotherapy and radiation. My mom had taken a job and worked a lot, and Jason and I were in school. Mindi was still in the honeymoon phase of her marriage, and we didn't see her much.

After this cycle of chemo and radiation, my dad's cancer once again went into remission. This time he looked drained, he had edema from the chemo drugs, and he was all puffy, in his face, hands, and feet, mostly. He slowly got better, but the treatment had taken a toll on him. This big, strong, tan man was now thin, pale, and his muscles had atrophied, but at least his sense of humor was back. We resumed family game nights, and he was cracking jokes. He would make fun of himself, poking his puffy skin and laughing that the indentation he made with his finger had stayed.

Life continued. I went to school, worked, and my dad continued to heal. I started to go out a little bit more with friends and searched for a boyfriend. Charlie finally asked me out with some coaxing from a co-worker. I liked him a lot, he was younger than me by a year and still in high school, but that didn't bother me. Charlie was tall, his dark hair feathered back, big brown eyes with long eyelashes, *wasted on a boy, in my opinion,* and a beautiful smile. We were friends at work, he was easy to talk to, and we had gotten to know each other over the past several months. We enjoyed the same music, TV shows, and movies. We talked about weekend plans, hobbies, and work. He was kind and listened to me.

On our first date, Charlie arrived on time at my front door and gave me a single red rose with baby's breath, tied with a pink bow. We decided to see a movie and go to a diner for a bite to eat afterward. As we sat in the booth, talking and sharing fries as he rubbed my back. He was sweet and caring. I told him about my dad and what he was going through.

"It's bizarre to see my dad like this. It's like he's a different person. I don't know what to say to him; we're not a close family that shares everything."

CHAPTER 2

"I think if you just do things for him or help out around the house, this will show him that you care. Sometimes we just can't find the words. When my grandpa was sick and dying, he told me that my grandma made small gestures. Going outside to get the paper and putting it by his breakfast in the morning or spraying his pillow with lavender before he went to bed so he could sleep better or warming a blanket for him when he was cold made a big difference to him."

"That's a good idea, Charlie. I'll try that."

"I'm here for you, Jess, whether you need to talk, cry, or need a hug."

"Thanks, Charlie, that means a lot." He put his arm around me and pulled me close, and kissed the top of my head. I breathed a sigh of relief.

After a couple of months of dating, Charlie wanted me to come over and meet his parents and his little sister. I agreed. Mrs. Cerny served a homemade cake. As we sat and enjoyed our cake and beverage, I had hot tea while Charlie and his parents had coffee, and his little sister had a glass of milk. The cake was moist and delicious. I asked Mrs. Cerny for the recipe.

Mr. and Mrs. Cerny were doctors, lovely people, but I could tell from the start that Mrs. Cerny did not like me. I don't know what she thought Charlie and I were doing, but all we were doing was dating and some kissing, nothing else. I felt like I was on the hot seat. She asked about my parents and seemed to disapprove that my father was a blue-collar worker, saying things like "I see." She asked if my parents had gone to college, to which I responded, no, my father was in the Army, and my mother did not go to college.

"What are you doing since graduating high school, Jessica?"

"I in community college and plan to go into healthcare."

"That's nice, dear."

Since I told her I wanted to go into healthcare, I thought that would earn me some brownie points with her. Nope.

Charlie and I continued dating. However, whenever we went out, it was like getting the third degree from Mrs. Cerny: "Where are you going? Who's all going? Be home by 10 p.m." Blah, blah, blah. I think if she had taken the time to get to know me, she would have known I wasn't some floozy after her little boy. I was sweet, and I genuinely enjoyed being with Charlie, but she had a way of making me feel unwelcome and dirty. After six months of dating, I decided to end things with Charlie. It was apparent his mom didn't like me, and her disapproval made me uncomfortable.

After work, Charlie and I met in the Dog House's parking lot, as we had done many times. "Charlie, I'm not sure how to say this, so I'm just going to say it. I think we should see other people." I felt horrible, and the look on his face made me feel even worse. "I just want to be friends." He quit the Dog House, and we never spoke again. I heard he had gotten a girlfriend pregnant right after high school but never married her. I bet his mom loved that! As for me, I plodded along at school and work, searching for Mr. Perfect.

CHAPTER 2

Cake Balls

Ingredients:

1 boxed cake mix, any flavor **OR** cake made from scratch.
1 can of prepared frosting to go with your box cake **OR** homemade frosting
Candy melts or chocolate chips

Directions:

Make cake according to box directions or your favorite homemade cake. Bake until a toothpick inserted in the middle comes out clean. Cool completely.

In a large mixing bowl, crumble up the cooled cake and add three-quarters of the frosting. Mix with beater until well blended and no longer crumbly. Shape into 1-1/2 or 2 inch balls. Cover cookie sheet with parchment paper or wax paper. Place balls on the parchment paper or wax paper. Put in the refrigerator for 1 hour. Cake balls should be firm.

Melt candy melts or chocolate chips in a bowl and microwave at 30-second intervals, stirring with a spoon in-between intervals until chocolate is melted.

With a fork or dipping tool, take one cake ball at a time and cover with melted chocolate. Return to a parchment paper or wax-covered cookie sheet until completely set. Decorate further if desired.

Enjoy! Jessica

CHAPTER 3

My father's cancer had returned once again; only this time, it was in his brain and liver. The prognosis was not good. I enjoyed spending time with my dad. When I was little, he would push Jason and me on the swing so high I thought we could touch the clouds. He took us to the zoo and the fair; I remember my tiny hand could barely wrap around his little finger when we walked. As I got older, we watched White Sox games, cooked together, played card games and board games, and had special lunch dates where we talked. I didn't want to see my dad dying. I didn't want to talk about it or even think about it. I kept myself distracted and out of the house. I plugged along at school, worked at the Dog House, and prayed. *God, please don't take my daddy away from me. I still need him.*

As the days went on, my father's cancer was not responding to the chemo treatments this time around. He spent most of his days in bed, unable to function. It was the sickest I had ever seen him. Christmas day arrived, and my father seemed to be in good spirits and was able to muster up enough energy to join us in the living room to open presents. He appeared to be happy and content being around his family today, and he even enjoyed some Christmas dinner at the table with us. I hoped his cancer was finally responding to treatment.

It was a cloudy, bitterly cold mid-January day, piles of snow on the ground from a recent snowstorm—typical Chicago winter weather. I was hard at work at the Dog House when

CHAPTER 3

my manager called me over and said that someone was here to see me. I turned and looked to see my Uncle Bill standing there. He didn't have to say anything; the look on his face said it all; my dad had passed away. Dazed, I clocked out and went to the breakroom to get my stuff. I exited the building without looking or speaking to anyone. I had parked my Camaro way in the back of the parking lot, and I walked as fast as I could to my car. I didn't even stop at my uncle's car, where my mom was waiting. I felt like I did in elementary school when the kids bullied me, I wanted to cry, but I didn't want anyone to see me. I sat in my car and let it warm up only a few minutes before leaving the parking lot. Once on the street driving towards home, I screamed "NOOOOOO," pounding my fists on the steering wheel. I was so angry. Why hadn't God listened to me when I begged for him not to take my father away from me? I still needed him. Didn't he know that? We all still needed him.

I don't even know how I made it home. Once there, I made my way to my bedroom. I stripped off my uniform and let it lay in a pile on my bedroom floor. I put on a fuzzy fleece top and sweatpants and crawled into bed. I laid in my bed, crying for hours while my mom was in the next room, ironing my dad's dress shirt and getting a suit and tie together that he would be wearing in his casket. I don't even remember what color the shirt was.

As much as it hurt to lose my father, there seemed to have been a massive weight lifted off my shoulders, somewhat of a relief. He wasn't suffering anymore, and I didn't have to see him weak and broken. I had prayed to God that he would heal my dad and cure his cancer, but why should he listen to me? We weren't church-going people. Did I even exist in his eyes? Was I *his* child? Why did I think I deserved anything from God? I knew I was a good person but was that enough?

The next couple of days were a blur. I hardly left my room, unable to eat, barely able to sleep, my head pounding with a headache. My mom and brother were out making arrangements, and the phone had been ringing all day, but I didn't pick it up. I didn't want to hear one more person say how sorry they were or if there was anything I needed. *Yes, I needed my dad, but I couldn't say that.* I'd say, "I'm fine." Finally, late in the afternoon, unable to take the phone ringing anymore, as it had been ringing every half hour since morning. I angrily answered it, "WHAT?!" A soft voice was on the other end, "I'm sorry to bother you. I'm calling from Peace and Love Funeral Home; we just need to know if we are to leave the deceased's beard on or shave it off?" I felt horrible that I did not answer the phone all day; after all, this woman was trying to do her job. In a small voice, I said, "Shave it off."

I don't remember much about the funeral at all except the look and smell of the flowers. My dad loved coral-colored roses, and we had a large arrangement made to go on top of the casket. People brought lots of food too, but I didn't feel like eating. I felt like everything was in slow motion, yet the day of the funeral flew by. I remember lots of people hugging me and giving my family their condolences, many of whom I didn't even know. I didn't know my dad knew so many people. He was young and probably the first of his friends to pass away. I don't recall anything else about that day, still dazed and in denial.

I resumed my classes and took the next week off of work. I sat on the couch quietly, thinking about my dad. I still couldn't eat, I didn't want to talk to anyone, and I was still crying. My best friend Kelly drove home from college for the weekend, came over to spend time with me, and gave me a box of my favorite Fanny May Trinidad Chocolates. She tried to talk to me, but I just didn't have anything to say. I sat on the couch, staring off into space, clutching a pillow sobbing. She didn't stay long.

My week off was up, and it was time to resume work at the Dog House. I had been back only a short while when one of

CHAPTER 3

my regular customers came in. He was an older Swedish man, not quite as old as my dad had been, probably in his forties, a nice guy who often flirted with me. He would say things to me like, "Do your eyes hurt? Because they are killing me" and make me blush. On this particular day, I was just not there mentally. Actually, I was having a lot of those days. Sven stepped up to the counter to order and said, "You've looked so sad lately. Is everything alright?"

I couldn't look him in the eye, and I said in a soft voice, "No, my dad died recently." "Oh, I'm so sorry, sweetheart," and he placed his hand on mine and gave it a little squeeze.

I felt like all my customers knew my secret just by looking at my face and my demeanor. It would take time to feel better. I don't think you get over the loss of your parent at such a young age, or ever. There is always a hole in your heart that you can never fill as hard as you try. There is always something—someone—missing.

For the next two years, I went through the motions of my daily routine. I was very angry with my dad for leaving us. We were still young, and my mom was a young widow at 50. I was mad at my dad for smoking for so long and endangering his health. Jason and I tried to help out my mom as much as possible with household expenses and chores. We were still young, and in college, Jason was 21, and I was 20. Jason was dating Amber, a girl he had met in his history classes. Jason had earned an academic scholarship to college, and all of his expenses were covered. I was still unclear on my path. I knew I wanted to do something in healthcare. I was working two, sometimes three temporary jobs, in addition to the Dog House, as I had to pay for college myself. I could only take a class here and there and didn't know if I would ever finish college.

I tried filling that hole. I was working, going to school, staying out way too late with my work friends, drinking and going to bars, and baking. Lots and lots of baking and eating my way through everything I baked. My best friend Kelly had changed schools and was in another state. My second best friend from high school, Julia, I lost contact with her after high school. I didn't know which college she had chosen. Feeling abandoned by my school friends, my Gram, and my dad, my life turned upside down, and I wondered what was in store for my new life. I was depressed and truly lost.

Mindi and Jeff were expecting their first child, which surprised me. Mindi does not have a maternal bone in her body and wanted a career, not a family. Jason and Amber were now serious about each other, and my mom worked a lot; I didn't see my family much. The house was quiet, empty most of the time, and I didn't want to be there.

As I had put on some weight since my Gram and dad's passing, I decided to start eating healthy and exercising. I was getting closer to my goal weight, but I was still chubby. I had finally picked a career, medical transcription. I finished the program and subsequently graduated with a certificate, not a degree, after five years. Medical transcription was in the healthcare field, and it settled in nicely with my long-term plan. I wanted to be a stay-at-home mom but still contribute to the family household financially. The best part about this job was I had the opportunity to work remotely. It was just what I wanted. I could work from home, and if my child was sick or had a play or sporting event, I could still be there for them. It was a win-win.

Shortly after graduating, I went job hunting. I applied for many transcription jobs, but they all required experience. How am I supposed to get experience if no one will hire me? Finally, about a month after graduation, I landed a part-time job in a private doctor's cardiology office, Dr. Mohammed. It was an okay job, I liked it, and I was learning a lot. I hit it off with my co-worker Katherine, we had a lot in common, and we became fast friends, spending time together in and out of the office.

CHAPTER 3

It was summer 1990, and I started to feel like I was coming out of my stupor and getting my life together. One thing was missing, though, a boyfriend—a serious boyfriend. Sure, I had dated in the past couple of years, here and there, nothing serious, no magic spark. They were guys that I had partied and hung out with, along with my Dog House co-workers. What I wanted most was to meet someone special. I was still on the chubby side, even though I was working on it. Nobody seemed interested in the chubby girl or the girl that didn't sleep around. I know I was old-fashioned, reserved, and quiet, definitely not the rowdy party girl. On one of our lunch dates, I remembered my dad had told me I was not to get pregnant out of wedlock, and I held up my side of the bargain so far. My search continued for Mr. Right.

Brookies

Step 1: Ingredients for the brownies:

1 cup butter
2 1/4 cups sugar
4 large eggs
1 1/4 cup unsweetened cocoa powder
1 teaspoon salt
1 teaspoon baking powder
1 teaspoon espresso powder (optional)*
1 tablespoon vanilla extract
1 1/2 cups all-purpose flour
2 cups semi-sweet chocolate chips

Step 2: Instructions for the brownies:

- Pre-heat oven to 350 degrees. Butter 9 x 13 baking dish.

- In a small saucepan over low heat, melt butter. Stir in sugar and continue cooking for 1-2 minutes, stirring constantly. Do not allow the sugar mixture to boil.

- Pour butter mixture into a large bowl or stand mixer, beat in cocoa powder, eggs, salt, baking powder, *espresso powder, and vanilla extract. Mix until well combined.

- Stir in the flour and chocolate chips until well combined.

- Spread the brownie batter into the buttered 9 x 13 dish and set aside.

Step 3: Ingredients for the cookies:

1/2 cup butter melted
1/2 cup brown sugar

CHAPTER 3

1/4 cup sugar
1 large egg
2 teaspoons vanilla extract
1 2/3 cup all-purpose flour
1 teaspoon baking soda
1/2 teaspoon salt
1 cup 60% bittersweet chocolate chips

Step 4: Instructions for the cookies:

- Add the melted butter, brown sugar, and white sugar to a large mixing bowl and stir well to combine.
- Stir in the egg and vanilla extract until smooth.
- Add the flour, baking soda, and salt to the mixing bowl and stir until well combined. Stir in the chocolate chips.
- Use a cookie scoop to drop cookie dough over the brownie batter. Use a buttered knife to swirl the batter and cookie dough together.
- Bake 25-30 minutes or until a knife inserted about an inch from the edge comes out almost clean.
- Cool before cutting into 16 squares.

Enjoy! Jessica

Chapter 4

On this particular steamy summer night, the restaurant and bar were bustling. Lorenzo Jr. asked me to help out in the bar area. Lorenzo Sr. had added karaoke night on Friday nights, and it was gaining popularity as the place was packed. I never liked karaoke; my shyness prevented me from intentionally seeking the spotlight. Tonight, a group of twenty-something guys and girls came in. They seemed to be co-workers, all dressed similarly in their royal blue polos and grey pants. It was someone's birthday, and they were celebrating together. They ordered a few pizzas and lots of drinks. Then they all started taking turns singing karaoke. Some were good, some not so good, and some were just plain awful. I noticed this one guy, in particular, as he swaggered through the crowd toward the stage. He had a honey-colored mane, a five-o'clock shadow, and striking blue eyes. His well-sculpted muscles rippled under his polo. He smiled and winked at the girls swooning around him. Distracted by this gorgeous specimen of a man, I bumped into a guy about my age, my tray of glasses crashing to the ground.

"Oh, my gosh, I'm sorry, are you okay? Are you cut or anything?"

"I'm fine," he said.

I apologized profusely; at least the beer mugs were empty, and I didn't spill anything on him. He looked at me and said, "Don't waste your time on that guy. He'll break your heart." *Whatever Mister Know It All.* I ignored what he said and

CHAPTER 4

proceeded to get a broom to clean up the glass shards and continued with my shift. I gazed at The Adonis throughout the night and avoided Mister Know It All.

I helped bring the pizza to the birthday party table. "Jessica?" One of the girls said. I turned and looked, and there was my old high school friend Julia.

"Julia, hello!" I was surprised to see her. "How are you? Are you living here? I lost track of you after high school. Where did you end up going to college?"

"I attended Duke University, and now I'm in medical school at the University of Chicago."

"Wow! Quite an accomplishment. I knew you'd choose a great career. You always had such high grades. What brings you back to the suburbs? Are you visiting family?"

"I came back to the 'burbs to spend time with family, friends, and former co-workers and celebrate one of their birthdays. I had worked with them at a bank during high school."

"What about you? What have you been up to?"

"Well, my dad suffered a heart attack in my senior year of high school. I'm not sure if you remember that. He recovered nicely, and then the next year, he was diagnosed with inoperable lung cancer and died a couple of years after that. I've been working and paying my way through college and just finished a medical transcription certificate program. I never was a good student."

"I'm sorry for your loss, Jessica," she said and looked down at her hands, clearly uncomfortable. I felt the need to lighten the mood.

"Thank you," I said as warmly as I could, "I'm getting through it."

Julia looked back up at me, hesitating at first, and then offered, "One of my friends here is having a party next weekend at an apartment complex clubhouse nearby. Do you want to go?"

"Yeah, that sounds like fun. I better get back to work."

"Okay, I'll call you during the week with the details, and we can catch up."

"Sounds great!"

Julia kept her promise and called me during the week, and we caught up. We were both in the medical field, so we had that in common. As usual, I had a busy week between the doctor's office and the Dog House. Finally, it was Friday night. I made great tips working that night and hoped it would be enough to buy a new outfit for my slimmer physique. I wanted to buy something special for the party Saturday night. I was helping to serve the pizzas tonight. Lots of families came in early on Friday nights, which I loved. It reminded me of my childhood, going out for pizza on Friday nights with my family. I fantasized about bringing my future kids here for pizza too. It would be our Friday night tradition. *Stop daydreaming, Jess; time to hustle; Friday nights are super busy.*

Bleep! Bleep! Bleep! The Saturday morning alarm clock rang way too early. I hit the snooze button a couple of times before getting up, showering, and going shopping for my new outfit. Why is it when you need something special to wear you can't find anything? And when you don't have an occasion or don't have the money, you find *a million cute outfits?* *I* was having a rough time finding just the perfect outfit and decided to go to one more store, Petite & Plus. I entered the store and started looking around. The saleswoman approached me and snarkily said, "Dear, I think you are on the wrong side. The plus-size clothes are over on *that* side of the store," pointing her bony finger in the direction of the plus-sized clothes. Her insensitivity stung. Whose brilliant idea was it to put a petite and plus-sized store together, anyway? I know I'm overweight, but next to a petite girl, I feel ten times bigger. I'm sure my face turned red as I was humiliated. Flashbacks of my bully Kimmy taunting me because of my weight blazed through my head. I didn't let on that the saleswoman got to me. I once again stuffed my feelings inside. I politely said to

CHAPTER 4

the saleswoman, "Oh, thank you, this is my first time in your store," and proceeded to the side of the store for us fatties.

I started browsing, rack after rack of cute clothes. I had a specific look I was after. Lo and behold, there it was! The outfit I had pictured in my mind. A white two-piece ensemble, a white beaded top, and a matching flowing skirt. It was gauze-like material and would be perfect for a summer party. I already had white sandals at home that would match perfectly.

Julia came and picked me up at my house at 8 p.m. and talked to my mom for a few minutes.

"Be good girls, don't drink and drive," my mom said as we headed out the door.

"Okay, mom."

As we drove to the party, we caught up.

"Are you seeing anyone, Julia?"

"No, not right now. I had a serious boyfriend during my first four years of college, and I thought we would eventually get married. He wanted to get married right away, and I wanted to finish my schooling first. I guess it just wasn't meant to be. What about you, Jessica? Dating anyone serious?"

"No, I've not been too lucky in finding a boyfriend. I've dated here and there, but my longest relationship has only been six months."

"Maybe you'll meet someone tonight."

"Maybe." I secretly crossed my fingers behind my back.

There were a lot of people in the clubhouse, and I started to feel anxious. Since I only knew Julia, I hoped we would stick together for most of the night. We received our red Solo cups and proceeded to the keg for a beer. I saw strawberry daiquiris and opted for one of those. Julia and I started to circulate. Out of the corner of my eye, I saw him—The Adonis—girls surrounding him, hanging on his every word. He was so good-looking I couldn't take my eyes off him. I walked closer to hear what he was saying that had the girls so enthralled.

My gaze was suddenly averted to the back corner of the clubhouse by a loud eruption of cheers. People were shouting. Chug! Chug! Chug! I looked over, and there was Mister Know It All playing some sort of game with shot glasses and quarters. He saw me and waved Julia and me over. Mister Know It All had wavy black hair, bluish-grey eyes, a beautiful smile, and tanned skin. Julia and I made our way closer to the table as he knocked off another opponent. I was observing how everyone was playing. He looked at me and said, "Hey, green eyes, wanna play?"

I smiled and said, "I never played before. What do I do?"

"You have to bounce the quarter on the table and into the shot glass. If you get it in, I have to drink. If you miss, you have to drink. Either chug a beer or drink a shot. What are you drinking?"

"Strawberry Daiquiri. I don't like beer and only have hard liquor when I can't taste it."

"Hey, Tommy," he shouted to his friend. "Bring over some watermelon shots."

I sat down, grabbed a quarter, and proceeded to bounce the quarter off the table into the shot glass, clink, plunk.

"Drink," I said and smiled. "Beginner's luck," I sassed to him.

"It's your turn again since you didn't miss it." I took the quarter, bounced it on the table, but this time missed the glass.

"Drink!" he teasingly commanded.

I downed one of the watermelon shots. *Yummy*. It didn't taste like alcohol at all.

Now it was his turn. He rolled the quarter down the bridge of his nose; it bounced on the table and clink, plunk right into the shot glass!

"Drink!" he said with a smile and a wink.

I downed another watermelon shot. After my opposition rolled the quarter off his nose and made it into the shot glass

CHAPTER 4

three times in a row, I had to call it quits. I was feeling buzzed, and I didn't want to be wasted an hour into the party.

"That's enough for me. Thanks for the game."

"Before you leave, green eyes… what's your name?"

"Jessica."

"I'm Vinny. Nice to meet you," and he shook my hand.

"Nice to meet you too, Vinny."

"Vinny, where is the bathroom?" Julia asked. He pointed to the other end of the room.

"I'll be right back, Jess."

"Okay, I'll wait over there on the couch." I needed to sit before I fell over and made an ass out of myself.

Vinny found me a minute later and joined me on the couch. I was sitting alone, gazing once again at The Adonis.

"Hey, Jess, enjoying the party?"

"Yep."

"How do you know Julia?"

"We went to high school together." "Who are you here with?"

He pointed and said, "That little short guy over there, Tommy."

"Ah," I replied. "How did you figure out you could roll a quarter off your nose and get it in the shot glass literally every time?"

"Oh, you know, hanging out with the guys horsing around, you start to do dumb shit. Then I just perfected it."

"I see."

I didn't know what else to say. Here was this good-looking guy talking to me, and I had no words in my head. My mind was completely blank. He started asking me many questions, where I was from, where I went to school and did I like Bruce Springsteen?

"I love the Boss!" I blurted out, "he's my all-time favorite."

"Do you want to go see him tomorrow?"

"Seriously? You have tickets?"

"Yes. I just don't have anyone to go with."

"Yeah, I'll go. How much are the tickets?"

"My treat. I'm going to need your phone number so I can call you tomorrow with the details." He pulled a piece of paper from his wallet, and I wrote my number on it, and he gave me his phone number, too. Then he leaned in really close and whispered in my ear with his hand on my knee, "My parents are out of town. Do you want to go back to my place?"

I was appalled, "I'm not that kind of girl." I said sternly, removing his hand from my knee. I was miffed but, at the same time, flattered. Vinny seemed like he expected that answer. He backed away a little and didn't press the question.

Julia appeared at that moment and announced that she had to go home, much to my relief. I stood up to join her, unsure about the moment that had just occurred between Vinny and me. I looked at him, and he smiled. "I'll call you tomorrow," he said

"Bye, Vinny."

"Bye, Jess. Drive safe, ladies."

As Julia drove me home, I grilled her about Vinny.

"How do you know Vinny?"

"Our families go to the same church, and I worked with him at the bank during high school."

"Is he a player?"

"Vinny?!" she laughed. "No, he is not a player. He comes from a good, hard-working blue-collar family. He's a good guy."

I was reeling with excitement, but I was also worried he wouldn't call me because I didn't go home with him. I could still smell his cologne as I drifted off to sleep, dreaming of Mr. Know It All.

CHAPTER 4

Banana Cake

Ingredients:

2 1/3 cups flour
1 2/3 cups sugar
1 1/4 cups ripe bananas (about 3-4)
2/3 cup shortening
2/3 cup buttermilk
3 large eggs
1 1/4 teaspoon baking powder
1 1/4 teaspoon baking soda
Nuts, optional

Directions:

Preheat oven to 350 degrees.

Beat all ingredients together. Pour into 9 x 13 pan sprayed with Pam or greased and floured. Bake 45-60 minutes until an inserted toothpick comes out clean.

Serve with vanilla frosting or warmed with a little bit of butter.

Enjoy! Jessica

Chapter 5

I stood in front of my closet, shuffling through my clothes, looking for the perfect outfit. It seemed so long ago that my closet was a fort where I sought refuge when my bullies picked on me. Now, it's just a closet. I decided to go with a white top with a tied knot on the side and blue jeans with a red bandana as a belt—I was thrilled with my smaller waist I could wear a bandana as a belt! And white sneakers. I hopped into the shower to get ready for my date with Vinny. As I was getting ready, I tried to decide if I should wear my hair up or down. I decided to wear my long wavy hair up in a ponytail tied with another red bandana; otherwise, my hair would be ten-feet wide from the humidity. I took my time getting ready and putting on my make-up. I like to look as natural as possible, but I just had to wear red lipstick. It looked striking with my fair complexion, dark brown hair, and light green eyes.

Vinny arrived right on time, wearing a bright florescent yellow t-shirt with a matching baseball cap and blue jeans.

"I heard they are videotaping the concert. If we make it into the video, I'll be easy to spot!"

I introduced him to my mom.

Then my mom started with the grilling, "Do you know how to get to the concert? Do you have a full tank of gas? Do you drive a reliable car? How long will the concert be? What time do you expect to be home?" *blah, blah, blah. My mom, the worry-wart.*

CHAPTER 5

Vinny very patiently and politely answered each one of my mom's questions. I quickly ushered him out the door before my mom could ask any more questions or embarrass me in some way.

We drove down to Soldier Field in Chicago. Vinny said, "We've got great seats, 28th row on the field in the center."

"Oh, my gosh! I can't believe I'm actually going to see the Boss, live, in-person!" I could hardly contain my excitement, not only for the concert but our date as well. We parked and headed to our seats and met the people around us, and chatted a bit. Before the show started, it began pouring buckets of rain. Within a matter of minutes, we were completely soaked! It continued to rain for about an hour, delaying the start of the concert. I said to Vinny, "We are going to look like drowned rats on this video."

He chuckled and said, "Well, you'll still look cute." I blushed and smiled.

Finally, the concert started, and it was amazing! The Boss played all my favorite songs. The saxophone was spectacular; it's such a sexy instrument, in my opinion. The Boss and the E-Street Band were having as much fun as we were. I was fully engaged and singing along with everyone else, not that anyone could hear me, which was a good thing. We were having a great time, dancing and laughing. We didn't care that we were soaking wet. I was able to snap some pictures of the Boss and band members, and Vinny. Bruce did four encores! FOUR! Nobody wanted it to end. Hands down, this was the best concert I had ever attended. We didn't care that we were soaked to the bone hours later; we had such a great time, a memorable first date for sure.

When the concert finally ended, it was past midnight. We headed out of the stadium to Vinny's sporty Monte Carlo SS. He put on the heat for the drive home as we were still wet, and I was shivering.

We talked about the concert all the way home. My ears were still ringing; I was tired and started to yawn.

"Am I boring you?"

"Oh no, not at all. I didn't get much sleep last night because I was so excited about going to the concert with you. I'm just tired, and I have to be up in a few hours to go to work."

"Yeah, I hear ya. I took a nap before the concert."

"Ah, a seasoned professional. I wish I had thought of that!"

Once we arrived home, he walked me to the door. It was too late to invite him in. We awkwardly stood there, not knowing what to say. Then at the same time, we blurted out, "I had a nice time tonight, thank you." A slight pause, "Jinx, you owe me a Coke!" and we laughed. Then he leaned in, cupped my cheek with one hand, and kissed me. It was the perfect kiss. Not too long, not too short, gentle, warm, and his lips were soft. I was entranced.

"May I call you again, Jess?"

"Yes, that would be great, Vin." My insides were all tingly, and my stomach was doing flip-flops. I'm sure I was blushing, but thankfully it was dark so that he couldn't notice.

My head was still in the clouds on Monday, and it was challenging, making it through the day at the doctor's office. I was distracted, thinking about Vinny and our enjoyable first date, smiling at the thought of him. I stayed in my office as much as possible and tried to concentrate on my work, which was futile—finally, lunchtime. I grabbed my co-worker/friend Katherine, and we went to the park to eat our lunch. I needed some fresh air and a walk. I told her all about my date with Vinny.

Katherine was petite with shoulder-length, dirty-blonde hair and hazel eyes. She was soft-spoken, intelligent, and was one of those people who were genuinely friendly. Katherine listened when I talked to her and gave sound advice. Above all, she had a strong relationship with God. I enjoyed spending

CHAPTER 5

time with her. She had a wonderful boyfriend, Jack, and I hoped that we would be double dating in the future.

I managed to make it through the day, and when I got home, there was a beautiful white basket full of red roses, tiny daisies, and baby's breath waiting for me. They were from Vinny, of course, with a note that read, *I had a great time last night, can't wait to see you again, Vinny*, XOXO. I changed my clothes and went to the park for my nightly run. My life was finally turning around; I could feel it.

Old Fashioned Dark Chocolate Cookie

Ingredients:

2 cups plus 2 tablespoons of all-purpose flour.
3/4 cup unsweetened dark chocolate cocoa powder
1 teaspoon baking soda
1/2 teaspoon salt
1 1/4 cups (2 1/2 sticks) butter, room temperature
2 cups granulated sugar
2 teaspoons pure vanilla extract
Coarse sugar, for rolling.

Directions:

- Sift together flour, cocoa powder, baking soda, and salt in a bowl, set aside.

- In the bowl of an electric mixer fitted with the paddle attachment, beat butter and sugar until light and fluffy, about 2 minutes. Add eggs and vanilla and mix until combined. Turn mixer speed to low and gradually add the flour mixture; beat until combined. Put the dough in a gallon-size plastic bag and flatten. Chill for about an hour.

- Preheat oven to 350 degrees; shape dough into 1 1/4 inch balls. Roll each ball into the coarse sugar. Place on baking sheets with parchment paper about 1 1/2 inches apart. Bake 10-12 minutes, rotating halfway through. Cool for 5 minutes and transfer to a cooling rack. Cookies may be stored between layers of parchment paper in an airtight container for up to one week.

Enjoy! Jessica

Chapter 6

Vinny and I started dating each other exclusively. Although I had dated other boys in the past, no relationship lasted longer than three months, except Charlie. I liked Charlie, but it was clear that his mother did not like me. I dated one boy after Charlie, just before Vinny briefly; I just wasn't into him. There were no butterflies, no spark. Dating Vinny, though, this relationship was different; I could feel it. When I thought of him, I smiled, and when I saw him, my heart skipped a beat. We had some different interests, and we also found we had a lot in common. He had a great sense of humor. He was always singing and happy. He knew how to enjoy life.

I headed over to Vinny's apartment to hang out. "Hey, Vin, let's play a game to get to know each other a little better. I made myself comfortable at one end of the couch and faced him on the other side of the couch. Each person gets to ask a question and the other person has to answer honestly. Then the person who asked the question has to answer the same question truthfully too."

"Okay, I'm game."

"I'll go first. Vin, what is your favorite color?"

"Blue, what's yours?"

"Depends. In cars, I like white. In lipstick, pink or red. I guess my overall favorite color, though, is purple."

"My turn. Jess, what's your favorite ice cream flavor?"

"Hmmm, I'm not a huge fan of ice cream, but I would have to say chocolate chunk brownie. What's yours?"

"Mint chocolate chip."

"My turn. Vin, do you like deep-dish pizza or thin crust pizza?"

"Definitely deep-dish."

"I like thin crust and the middle pieces."

"Follow-up question," Vin said. "What makes for a great pizza, the sauce, or the crust?"

"Hands, down the crust, it has to be buttery and flaky."

"I agree with you on that, Jess."

"What qualities turn you off in a girl?"

"I guess an unkempt appearance, wears too much make-up, a girl who swears a lot and is disrespectful to others." I thought about the first night we met, and he asked me to go home with him. Was he testing me? He certainly had traditional ideas around feminity, and I fit right in.

What turns you off in a guy?"

"A guy who smokes or does drugs, arrogance, a disrespectful guy. Oh, and tickling."

"Tickling? You don't like to be tickled?"

"No! I do not, so don't even try it!"

"Why don't you like to be tickled?" He had an impish grin on his face.

"Because I'm super ticklish. You will tickle me, and I'll be laughing trying to fend you off, and then it will happen, I'll toot, and it will be mortifying! Then for years to come, you will bring it up at the most inappropriate time for the rest of our lives and say, do you remember when I was tickling you, and you tooted? You'll think this is hilarious, and I'll be humiliated all over again. So please don't do it!

He grabbed my hand; my eyes widened as I tried to wiggle out of his grasp.

"Vincenzo Fontana, I'm not kidding!" I squealed.

CHAPTER 6

He lifted my hands to his lips and gently kissed them. "I promise I will never do anything to embarrass you." The tone of his voice made me believe him.

"Okay, my turn," he said. "This one is crucial. Are you a Cubs fan or White Sox fan?"

Being a Chicagoan all my life, I knew how important this question was. You see, in Chicago, you can only cheer for one baseball team, the Chicago Cubs, or the Chicago White Sox – never both. My answer could put a strain on our relationship if we disagreed.

"I'm a Sox fan," I said.

"Oh!" he clutched his chest, faking a heart attack, and fell back into the couch. "Thank God! I'm a Sox fan too!" *Whew, what a relief. My dad would be happy if he were still around, that is.* "I see many ballgames in our future, Jessica."

"My turn." I thought about bringing up this question so early in our relationship. I hesitated and then decided I'm not getting any younger and better to know now than a year into the relationship. "Vin, do you ever want to get married and have children?"

"Of course, I want to get married someday and have lots of kids running around."

"Define lots," I said.

"I'm thinking four to six."

"I want lots of kids too. I can't think of a better experience than being a parent."

"I agree, a family is essential, and I want a big one. I want to teach my children the stuff my parents taught me. My dad taught me how to do minor repairs around the house. My mom taught me how to cook and clean, I'm not great at it, but I can do it. We had to work for what we wanted. I think it's important for parents to teach their children to be a productive part of the community."

"I completely agree with you, Vin."

There was a brief pause; Vinny was in deep thought for a few seconds. "Hey, Jess, do you want to go to the festival next weekend? I'd like you to meet some of my friends."

"Sure, a lot of my friends will be there too, and you can meet my friends also. I'll be working most of the day in the Dog House food tent. I can meet you in the evening after work."

"Sounds like a plan." I was excited he wanted me to meet his friends, and I wanted him to meet mine too.

We ate our way through the various food tents. It was time to meet our friends at the beer and wine tent and listen to music. He introduced me to his friends, and I introduced him to my friends. The funny thing was, a lot of our friends already knew each other. Vin and I couldn't believe that we had not met each other sooner. Vin and I spent every day together after the festival. We worked around our schedules to see each other. Vin joined me when I went running or walking. He enjoyed playing basketball with the guys at the same park where I ran. We met up after our activities and would sit on the bleachers with our frozen custard from the concession stand and talk until the park closed.

As we spent more time together, I left little love notes around his apartment or his car for him to find. I enjoyed baking for him too. It felt like we had known each other our whole lives. I felt comfortable with him. I was falling for this guy. I had never felt this way with any of the boys I had dated. Charlie came the closest.

One evening while watching basketball on TV, he turned to me and said, "Jess, I want you to meet my family."

"Really?"

"Yes. We've been dating for a few months, and I think it's time. We are having a family BBQ next Sunday after church. I would like you to join us."

"Okay, that sounds like fun." *Hopefully, this will go better than when I met Charlie's parents.* "I'll bring some cookies."

"My dad would love that; he loves sweets."

CHAPTER 6

"Hey, Vin, why don't you come over Saturday night and help me bake the cookies?"

"Sure, but only if I can be the official cookie taster," he said with a smile.

"Deal."

Sunday morning came. I wrapped my silver cookie platters with cellophane and curling ribbon – presentation is everything. Vinny picked me up at my house, and we drove to his parent's house. As we pulled into the driveway, I had a nervous tremble in my stomach, and my mouth was dry. *Don't blow this, Jess, just be yourself.* Vinny helped me with the cookie platters as we walked up the driveway, and he escorted me to the backyard, where his father was manning the grill.

"Mom, Dad, this is my girlfriend, Jessica Novak. Jessica, these are my parent, Franco and Rose Fontana."

"Hello, it's very nice to meet you, Mr. and Mrs. Fontana. Thank you for having me. I baked some cookies for you, chocolate chip, and Bohemian Almond Crescent cookies."

"Oh, Bohemian Almond Crescents are my favorite," said Rose. "I'm Bohemian. Are you Bohemian, Jessica?"

"Yes, and German. Where would you like me to put these?"

"Right over here, follow me," his mom said, taking one of the platters and asking me about my Czech roots as we walked.

"She's cute," Vinny's dad said.

"Yes, and she's sweet too, dad. I really like her."

"You must since this is the first girl you ever brought home for us to meet."

Vinny introduced me to the rest of the family. "Jessica, I want you to meet my brother and sister. This is my brother Gino and his wife, Heather."

"Hi, nice to meet you," we shook hands.

"And this is my sister Gina, her husband Ken, and my nephew Ryan and niece Brittany."

"Hi, it's nice to meet all of you. Your children are adorable."

"Oh, thank you, they are a handful at this age." Off she went to tend to her toddlers.

We enjoyed the day playing cards, talking, and eating. His mom shared embarrassing stories of Vinny growing up, and we laughed a lot. They were genuinely gracious people. They reminded me of how my family used to be. With my dad gone, we didn't seem to get together as much, and I missed it. I wanted to be part of Vinny's family.

As the evening came to an end, Vinny drove me home and walked me to my door, and kissed me goodnight. "I had a lovely time Vinny. Your family is very kind."

"They really liked you, Jessica." A sense of relief came over me.

"I really liked them too, Vin. I can't wait to see them again."

We started spending more time at Vinny's parent's house. After our evening walk, we would hang out with his parents and play cards or sit around and talk.

The next day I arrived at Vinny's apartment after work to find him packing. "Why are you packing? Where are you going?"

"I'm sorry, Jess, I have to go out of town in a couple of days for a last-minute business trip. Steve, my co-worker who was supposed to go, had an emergency appendectomy. I have no choice. I have to go. I'm going to miss you, Jess."

"Oh, no. I'm going to miss you too, Vin." I said, pressing my hand to my abdomen. We spent all of our free time together the days leading up to his trip.

The night before his trip, I went over to Vinny's apartment to help him finish packing and, of course, to spend as much time with him as possible. Before I left for the evening, Vin said, "I have something for you."

"What is it?" I said with excitement. He went into his closet and pulled out a box, and handed it to me.

"This is for when you are missing me, and you need a kiss."

CHAPTER 6

I unwrapped the box, and inside was a big jar of Hershey Chocolate Kisses. "Oh, my gosh, that is so cute, Vin." "I'll probably eat these the first day you are gone. I'm going to miss you so much."

"I'm going to miss you too, Jess." He leaned in and kissed me like a soldier going off to war. He walked me to my car. "I'll see you next week when I get back."

"Okay," I said softly. "Have a safe trip, and call me when you get home."

"I will. Goodnight."

"Goodnight." I got in my car and drove home with tears in my eyes.

The week Vinny was gone dragged on at a snail's pace. I could not believe how much I missed him. My mom referred to me as a lovesick puppy as I moped around the house. It was then that I realized that this relationship was different. I was in love with Vinny. I wanted to be with him every day. I missed him so much I could hardly stand it; my heart ached. When he got home, I told him just that.

"Vin, I missed you so much this week." I hesitated and thought to myself if I should say those three words. Is it too soon? Would I scare him off? What if he doesn't say it back? Oh, my gosh, WHAT IF HE DOESN'T SAY IT BACK?! For once in your life, Jessica, stand up for yourself and tell him how you feel. I looked him right in the eye and said, "I love you."

He smiled and said, "I love you too, babe, and I missed you too." We never spent another day apart unless he had an occasional business trip.

I was curious about church, and Vinny's faith was essential to him, and Vinny was important to me. I started attended Vinny's church with him and his family. I enjoyed it and the way it made me feel happy and part of a community. I loved that Vinny, his brother, and his father all tried to out-sing each other and be the loudest. His dad always won. I attended classes and became a member of the Lutheran Church, and was baptized as an adult.

We dated four years before Vinny proposed. He finally popped the question the Friday night before Valentine's Day at one of our favorite restaurants. Vinny got down on one knee and gave me a pink conversation heart that read, *marry me?* As I looked into his eyes as he said, "Jessica, I fell for you the first day I saw you when you crashed into me at the Dog House. I couldn't keep my eyes off you, but I chickened out and didn't ask you out. Then fate brought us together the very next weekend. I had a second chance and asked you to the concert. I can't think of anyone else I want to go with to concerts and White Sox games. Jessica, you are my best friend, and I love you. I want to spend the rest of my life with you. Will you marry me and be my wife?" and then gave me a white conversation heart that read, *say yes.* I replied excitedly, "Yes, I will marry you, Vinny!" and he slipped an oval solitaire diamond ring on my finger. The patrons of the restaurant who were silently witnessing our private moment clapped for us.

CHAPTER 6

Bohemian Almond Crescent Cookies

Ingredients:

1 cup butter
1/2 cup confectioners' sugar
1 teaspoon vanilla
2 cups sifted flour
1 cup chopped or ground almonds

Directions:

Preheat oven to 350 degrees.

Cream butter and blend in sugar and then vanilla. Add the flour gradually, stirring until smooth after each addition. Stir in nuts.

Dip fingers into flour and then shape into crescents or roll out the dough and use a small juice glass rim to cut crescent shapes from cookies (half of the rim, start at the edge of the dough).

Place on an ungreased cookie sheet and bake for 15-20 minutes. When slightly cool, roll in additional confectioners' sugar.

Enjoy! Jessica

Chapter 7

Vinny and I bought our first house a couple of months before our wedding. A blue, fifteen-hundred square foot raised ranch with a spacious fenced-in yard, a good starter home. We managed to stay within mom's rule that no one in the family could live more than twenty minutes from someone else. We lived fifteen minutes from mom, fifteen minutes from Mindi, and twenty minutes from Jason.

In early spring, we took our vows in the Lutheran Church with our best friends at our side. Katherine was my matron of honor, and Tommy was Vinny's best man. Candlelight adorned the pews at our church on a Friday night in the spring. It was perfect. The reception was rather large, with 150 guests, held at a hotel and convention center close to the church. Our guests dined on their choice of prime rib, chicken Kiev, or salmon with a twice-baked potato and steamed veggies. Our wedding cake was gorgeous. Three heart-shaped tiers of chocolate cake with white buttercream frosting, accentuated with deep-purple buttercream roses and piping, with five smaller heart-shaped cakes surrounding it. We worked hard to pay for the wedding ourselves, and we had a fantastic time celebrating our big day with family and friends. After dinner, I walked around and thanked our guests for coming and chatted with them while Vinny danced the night away.

We honeymooned in Florida and talked more about our future. We wanted to start a family right away, four to six kids. We agreed that we would not spoil our kids with lots of

CHAPTER 7

material things. When they were old enough, they would do chores to earn money and save for what they wanted; after all, that's how our parents raised us. We wanted a family that supported each other and had fun together. We wanted to go on family vacations and other outings. We both agreed, getting along, laughing, and loving each other is what family is all about. It's the most meaningful lesson we wanted to teach our children.

The honeymoon ended, and it was time to start our married life together, still blissfully in love and optimistic. On Vinny's first day back to work, he found out his company was relocating to North Dakota. He could keep his job if he transferred to North Dakota. We had just bought a house, and after we discussed it for a long time, he opted not to go and was out of a job. I was now working full-time at the doctor's office. I certainly didn't earn enough to pay our mortgage, and I had quit the Dog House just before our wedding. There it was, our first speed bump as a married couple. We banned together, Vinny kept on task, looking for work, and I started baking for extra cash. We would later find out that this was one of the easier bumps to get over in our marriage. The thought of having children was put on hold for now.

After six months of job searching, Vinny interviewed at a software company in downtown Chicago and accepted the job. He commuted to and from the 'burbs to the city, which made for some very long days. He took many naps on the weekends. We decided to try and start a family. All our brothers and sisters were well on their way to completing their families. Vinny's brother Geno and sister, Gina, had completed their families, as well as my half-sister, Mindi. Jason and Amber were married the year before us and were expecting their first child. It was our turn to start trying.

Months went by, and I was still not pregnant. It seemed like every time we went to a family gathering or work, someone was pregnant, and we still were not. Every family gathering, every holiday, I was asked, are you pregnant yet? I was polite and said no, not yet. I was puzzled and sad at the same time; *why weren't we getting pregnant?* My inability to get pregnant went on for two tormenting years before I decided to look for medical assistance. I went to my gynecologist first. The doctor told me I was perfectly healthy, and maybe I just needed some help. He prescribed infertility medication. The medication made me very ill, and I thought I might be pregnant, but then Aunt Flo showed up. My doctor took me off the drug. I decided to check out other methods for getting pregnant. I researched acupuncture and found that acupuncture increased fertility by reducing stress, increasing blood flow to the reproductive organs, and balancing the endocrine system. I started a search for an acupuncturist who specialized in infertility. I found one a few towns away and scheduled an appointment. Dr. Duke was a chiropractor, certified in acupuncture, and had been practicing for years and claimed that he had a 100% success rate with his infertility patients. Dr. Duke explained the procedure and suggested I take certain supplements and eat a healthy diet.

After Dr. Duke answered all of my questions, I decided to proceed with treatment. I was stuck with needles all over my body three times a week for a year, which was not covered by insurance and was quite expensive. I ate healthily and took the supplements he suggested—still, no pregnancy. Aunt Flo visited every month, much to my disappointment. Vinny and I decided to give it a rest, not think about it so much. Maybe if I stopped treatment for a while, I would stop obsessing over baby names and nursery room themes and about not being pregnant. I was hoping it would happen naturally. That didn't seem to work either. Month after month after month Aunt Flo continued to show up. *Why was it so easy for some and so difficult for us?* In the meantime, it seemed like everyone was popping out babies every time they sneezed. *When the*

CHAPTER 7

timing is right, it will happen. Just relax, Jess, it will happen, I told myself.

A few years later, Vinny went through another job change, necessitating an even longer commute, this time to Chicago's northern suburbs. I also changed jobs when the doctor I worked for moved to another state. I found a medical transcription job where I worked remotely, and it was perfect. The entire reason I went into my field was to work at home and be with my children when they needed me. I found that I really enjoyed working at home, and once again, we tried to start a family. All our siblings' families were complete, no more babies for them. I wasn't getting any younger, so I decided to look into an infertility specialist. At that time, in Illinois, companies did not have to carry infertility insurance; it was considered an elective procedure. Neither of our jobs offered coverage for infertility treatments. Children were on hold once again while we researched alternatives.

Now in our mid-thirties and feeling secure in our jobs, life was going well, except for our childlessness. We had been in the house for eight years and decided to look for a new home. Because, as you know, whenever you move into a new home, you have a baby. We found a new subdivision just starting construction on what had previously been farmland. It was only ten minutes from where we lived now. We would be out of mom's distance rule by ten minutes, but she was thrilled for us. We had a semi-custom Georgian home built with four bedrooms, two and a half bathrooms, a big kitchen, home office, family room, dining room, living room, full basement, and a three-car garage directly across from the elementary school. We had fun picking out everything; the lot, the exterior brick, the cabinets, and interior light fixtures. This home would certainly be large enough to accommodate the family we were anticipating having. With all the young couples moving into the subdivision with small kids and more on the way, I was hoping to join them soon.

I daydreamed about making pancakes on Sunday morning before church, baking cookies with my kids during the holidays, and having fresh baked cookies for them when they got home from school. Also, we would have the family barbeques in the summer to be together or celebrate a birthday. The marvelous smell of turkey roasting in the oven on Thanksgiving Day and decorating the Christmas tree as a family, followed by hot cocoa and a Christmas movie. I dreamed of big family Christmas gatherings with lots and lots of presents. I thought about the silly and fun holiday traditions we would have, the games we would play, and the family Christmas card we would send. Oh, how this was my happy place!

I had fun picking out the colors for the kid's rooms, one pink, one blue, and one lavender. I picked a rubber ducky theme for their bathroom. I painted the bathroom walls light blue with a rubber ducky wallpaper border, matching rug, shower curtain, and accessories. It was the first room completed in the new house, and it was adorable. I couldn't wait to give my children their baths and teach them how to brush their teeth, then tuck them in bed and read them a bedtime story. I daydreamed a lot about having little feet scampering about the house and the laughter that would follow. Children's laughter is my favorite sound. However, that was not my reality. I worked at home all day by myself in this big silent house. I sometimes sat in the lavender room with a crib and a rocking recliner that Amber gave to me since she and Jason were done having children and cried.

Vinny's company was downsizing, and once again, he lost his job. He had gained a lot of management experience, so this time he was only out of work for a couple of months. He found a job in the next town, a twenty-minute commute. While his career was going well, mine was not. Technology completely changed my career, took most of it away. I was now making a third of my usual pay. I didn't have any other skills. I had to stick it out and get paid less for the same amount of work,

CHAPTER 7

which was stressful and a tough adjustment, mentally and financially. I worked a lot of weekends and holidays just for the extra money my boss was paying, trying to make up for the lost wages. Vinny did all the landscape work on the weekends during the summer and took many naps; he always seemed tired. Despite his tiredness, during the winter, he decided to finish our full basement. He made me a craft room down there, where I could have my mom and my friend Katherine over to scrapbook when I was not working. I did a lot of baking and crafting for supplemental income.

We were friendly with our neighbors and, at first, spent a lot of time socializing with them. It was a good group of friends. All of them either had small children or were pregnant. We attended their kid's birthday parties for the first couple of years. We ate dinner together a lot, too, taking turns hosting in each other's backyard on the patio. Everyone would bring their prepared food, and we sat and ate together and talked. After we were done eating, the kids played. One neighbor built a movie screen out of a bedsheet and PVC piping and used a laptop and projector to project the movie onto the "screen." We gathered at their house for Friday night, "movie night" during the summer. We brought our chairs, drink, and snack. The kids were in their PJs, and we watched a kid's movie first. When that movie was over, the moms would take their kids home, tuck them in bed, and come back with a baby monitor. The adults watched a PG or R-rated movie. Often, the women didn't come back after tucking their kids into bed, and I was there with all the men. At first, I was okay with it, but then I started to feel awkward. I felt like they wanted to talk about guy stuff, but since I was there, they didn't or couldn't. Some weekends the men played cards together, rotating houses each time, and the women stayed home with the kids while I stayed home alone. After a couple of years, we were no longer invited to the birthday parties, their parents saying, "We are only inviting other parents." One neighbor told me that she forgot about Vinny and me because we didn't have children; we were not at the school functions with the other parents, and we didn't have children for her children to play together. It was hard to see our neighbors gathered together in their backyards for kid's birthday parties and not be invited. Vin and I were becoming invisible in our neighborhood.

We were getting older, in our late thirties, and still wanted children. After a lengthy discussion, we decided to look into adoption. While searching the internet, I found an adoption agency in Texas. The Hope Adoption Agency's website indicated they had several babies available for adoption. I called and spoke to the receptionist and requested an information packet. It arrived a few days later with lots of paperwork to read and fill out. The one thing that stood out to us was that the adoption prices were based on the child's race. Caucasian, Asian, half Caucasian/half Hispanic, or half-Caucasian/half Asian infants were the highest cost. The next price tier was for full Hispanic, half Hispanic/half African-American, and American Indian. The lowest cost was for full African- American. That did not sit well with us.

Nevertheless, I talked to one of the caseworkers on the phone and told her I had all the paperwork filled out and asked what the next steps were. I inquired how many of the children that were on the website were still waiting to be adopted. She informed me that my next steps would be to pay the fee for whatever race of child we would feel would be best suited to our family. Then to get a home study and start taking all the required classes and start the required reading. She then indicated that all the children pictured on the website had been adopted, and it would be a two-year wait. I felt gut-punched, and I was angry. I told her if the babies were no longer available for adoption, they should take their pictures off the website. It gave prospective adoptive parents false hope by showing the photographs and stating they had

CHAPTER 7

many babies waiting to be adopted. In the end, we decided not to go with the Texas agency.

I spoke with my friend Katherine often- as she and her husband were also having fertility issues. She was my only friend I knew wanted children but had problems conceiving, just like me. We had many, many phone calls over the years. She had told me about a Lutheran-based adoption agency, Little Darlings, which was close to my house. She and her husband had looked into the agency. When it came down to it, Katherine's husband didn't want to adopt. He wanted a biological child. Vin and I still wanted to be parents; it didn't matter if the child was biologically ours. We would love him or her, no matter what. Although I still yearned to be pregnant and go through the experience, it wasn't happening. We decided to look into the agency. I called Little Darlings and reserved a spot for orientation later that week. I had more questions, and the receptionist transferred me to the director. I asked the director what they charged for adoption over the phone, and she said it is based on your income, not to exceed $40,000.

Prices were not based on race. That was a plus in my book. I asked about age, as we were on the older side, thirty-six. The director also said we were still within their parameters, and we would move to the top of the list because of our age--another plus. The $40,000 adoption fee was a lot of money, and we didn't have it. I mean, who has $40,000 lying around? People think childless people have lots of money, but we don't. Most of us have spent loads of money out-of-pocket on medical procedures that didn't even work. We would figure out the financing later.

We arrived at the adoption agency, notebooks in hand, for the seminar. There were a lot of couples there, and we were definitely the oldest. We sat and listened to the speaker with information about the process. Next, a couple who adopted through the agency spoke about their experience and how accommodating the staff had been. They showed us pictures of their child, now a pre-teen. Finally, a woman who had been put up for adoption as a newborn spoke. She had a loving adoptive family, and she knew her birthmother and had a relationship with her. Vin and I had discussed at length about being open and honest with our adopted child from the beginning. He or she would know that we adopted them. We were hoping for a birth mother who would want to keep communication lines open should her son or daughter want to know her and have a relationship with her in the future.

In the end, Vinny and I looked at each other and knew this was the agency for us. The director came up to give her closing speech and then said, "At this time, we do not have any openings for adoptive parents. We only take on so many adoptive parents per month, and with the economic recession, births have been down. Please feel free to keep in touch and check back at a later date." Talk about getting our hopes up and then squashing them! I was getting so depressed and angry about the whole situation. My mother-in-law would say, "If it's God's will, then it will happen." Why didn't God want us to have a child?

I know I was probably more than a little sensitive about the situation as the months passed. I would hear shocking stories on the news about mothers killing their children, or abuse and neglect by a parent, or leaving a newborn in a dumpster. I thought to myself, why would God give them children and not me? The faith I had was dimming, and I was starting to feel depressed. Although I was genuinely happy for everyone in my life who was pregnant, I was wondering what was wrong with me. Did I do something wrong? Am I being punished for something? Would I be a bad mother? Being a mom was the only thing I've ever wanted to be, and I knew in my heart I would be a great mom, and Vinny would be a great dad. Why can't I have a baby? Why didn't God want us to be parents?

We accepted an invitation to a birthday party for Tommy's son, who was turning one. He and Vinny were chatting away

CHAPTER 7

at the party. I was within earshot but not right next to Vinny. Tommy was gushing over how much he loved being a dad, all the cute things his son does, and how fascinating the experience has been so far. Then he said to Vinny, "What about you, man? Are you and Jess going to have kids soon? You're not getting any younger, you know." Vinny laughed a little and said, "We're working on it, but we are having problems getting pregnant." To which Tommy replied, "Looks like you married a lemon!" *OUCH!* I heard him say that, and it was like I was punched in the stomach and stabbed in the heart all at the same time. Was that what everyone was thinking? Did Vinny think that?

I went over to the cake table to eat my feelings away. A little girl was standing there with her mom, helping to pass out pieces of birthday cake. The mom reached for a piece of cake to give to me, and her little girl sneezed on it. She handed it to me anyway, as if nothing had happened. *Ewww, gross!* I politely said, "I prefer a piece that hasn't been sneezed on." The woman stared at me, both with surprise and what I thought was smug disdain as if I didn't understand some parental code that allowed for eating food contaminated by children. And I suppose I didn't. I then decided to pass on the cake altogether and walked away.

Without children in the house, I was feeling lonely. Our house was big and empty, and I was home all day by myself. After much discussion, we decided to rescue a puppy. We decided on an Italian Greyhound. I wanted a lap dog, a little dog I could snuggle. We found an Italian Greyhound rescue in Wisconsin and headed up for a visit the very next weekend. I fell in love with a little grey and white male. He was very playful, utterly obsessed with my shoelaces, and liked to be held and to give kisses. He was the one. We filled out the paperwork, headed home, and waited excitedly for our approval. It only took a couple of days for the Italian Greyhound rescue group to approve us. After receiving the approval phone call, we went to the pet store and bought a dog crate, a bed, a ton of toys, some treats, bowls, a leash, collar, and a little doggie White Sox jersey with a matching bandana. This little pup would be all set to sit on daddy's lap and watch the ball game with him.

We headed back to Wisconsin to pick up our pup the next weekend. On the ride home, I sat in the back with our new family member, and we snuggled all the way home. He was such a little love bug. Vin and I discussed names. Since he was so small, only seven pounds, we decided to name him Pip Squeak. Pippy for short. I finally had a warm tiny body with which to snuggle and play. Pippy and I developed a strong and loving bond; I absolutely adored him and doted on him. He followed me everywhere—a classic Velcro dog. I even starting baking dog treats just for him. Pippy appeased my mothering instinct, at least for the time being.

I called Katherine to tell her about the good news.

"Hello?"

"Hi, Katherine, it's Jess. It's a boy!" I shouted.

"Hi, Jess. You're having a baby?"

"Oh, no, sorry, I wish. We adopted a puppy, an Italian Greyhound. I can't wait for you to meet him. He is a sweet little guy. We named him Pippy."

"Aw, congratulations. I was going to call you this weekend." She hesitated, "I went to the doctor, and they found a lump in my breast. I have breast cancer."

"What? Oh, no, Katherine, I'm so sorry to hear this. Are you okay? Is it in your family?"

"Yeah, I'm doing okay. My aunt had breast cancer and, unfortunately, died at an early age. I'm going to have a double mastectomy, chemo, and radiation starting next week."

"Wow. That's a lot. Is there anything I can do for you and Jack?"

"I'll let you know. Jack's parents are helping out."

CHAPTER 7

"Okay, well, if you need anything, and I mean anything, just let me know."

"I will. Thank you. Are you and Vinny still looking to adopt?"

"Yes, but we had no luck at the adoption agency. They are full."

"Grace is a friend of mine from church. She is pregnant, and she asked me if I wanted to adopt her baby. Jack doesn't want to adopt, and in light of my recent cancer diagnosis, I don't think I would even try to discuss it with him. I thought of you and Vinny. Do you want me to give your name and contact information to Grace?"

"Hold on a sec Katherine."

Vinny was sitting across from me. I put my hand over the phone to not talk into Katherine's ear while I asked Vinny his thoughts. "Vin, Katherine's friend, is pregnant and looking to give the baby up for adoption. Katherine thought of us. What do you think? Can she give her friend our name?"

"Of course! Get some details about the situation, the father of the baby, drug use, etc."

"Hi, Katherine?"

"Yes, I'm still here, Jess."

"Okay. Yes, you may give Grace our information. Do you know anything about the father?" I'm so excited!"

"No, it was a one-time thing. She met him at a party. She doesn't even know his last name.

"Oh, that's too bad. Any drug use or anything like that?"

"No, she doesn't do things like that. She is in her thirties and single. She doesn't think she can raise a baby alone, and in her culture, her family would disapprove."

"Oh, wow, that's heartbreaking."

"I'll give Grace your information. I hope she reaches out. You and Vin would make great parents."

"Thanks, Katherine. Please let me know when you will feel up to having visitors after your surgery and chemo and radiation treatments."

"Okay, Jess, I will. Have a good evening."

"You too. I love you, Katherine; bye."

"Me too, Jess, bye."

As I hung up the phone, I was conflicted. I was sad to hear Katherine's cancer news, but at the same time, I was happy that maybe we would be adopting Grace's baby.

CHAPTER 7

Refrigerator Cheesecake

Graham cracker crust:
Ingredients:

1 1/2 cups graham cracker crumbs (or 12 full sheets crushed)
1/3 cup granulated sugar
6 tablespoons butter, melted.

Prepare graham cracker crust:

Preheat oven to 350 degrees.

Mix the graham cracker crumbs, sugar, and melted butter in a small bowl.

Pour graham cracker mixture into an 8" to 9.5" pan and press firmly in the bottom of the pan and a little bit up the sides of the pan.

Bake for 10 minutes and allow to cool.

Refrigerator cheesecake:
Ingredients:

8 oz package of cream cheese, softened
14 oz can of sweetened condensed milk
1/3 cup lemon juice
1 teaspoon vanilla.

Directions:

Beat cream cheese until fluffy, add condensed milk and beat until smooth, add lemon juice and vanilla and mix a little more. Pour into crust and chill for three hours. Leave plain

MY SECRET GRIEF

and sprinkle a little bit of graham cracker crumbs on top or top with fruit pie filling if desired; my favorite is blueberry!

** You can add chocolate chips into the cream cheese mixture before pouring into the crust. Omit fruit topping if you do this.

Enjoy! Jessica

Chapter 8

Vinny came home from work bursting through the door. "Jessica?"

"I'm upstairs," I yelled down to him. "I'll be down in a minute."

"Hurry, I have good news!"

I rushed downstairs. "What's going on?"

"My co-worker Steve and I were talking about kids. I told him how we were having problems getting pregnant, and he said he and his wife were trying for a second child and were having problems too. Our boss overheard us, and after some discussion, decided to look into getting infertility insurance for us!"

"Wow! That's kindhearted of him."

"Since we only have five employees, three of whom have finished having children. I agree it's generous of them to help us out."

The next week Vinny brought home the paperwork, and we looked it over together. I was making less money; finances were tight. The plan didn't pay for everything. We still had our share to pay. Insurance didn't cover the infertility drugs, and they came with a hefty price of $5,000 per cycle of IVF to harvest my eggs. Ultimately, we decided this was our last chance to have a biological child. We had an opportunity, and we had to take it. We would figure out the money later.

We found the best doctor in our area, Dr. Andrews. She was accepting new patients, and we were lucky enough to schedule an appointment with her even though we had to wait a month, as she was booked solid. She had a good track record of success, helping couples start a family.

We went for our consultation, and it was not as promising as we had hoped. Now in our early forties, and Dr. Andrews was treating me like I was ninety. She told me I might not have many eggs left, and those I do have may not be viable. We would both have to go through a series of tests to ensure everything was in good order. I felt hopeful. We complied with all the tests ordered, and we got them done as soon as possible.

All my tests came back clear except that I had an anteverted uterus, but she told us it shouldn't be a problem. Vinny, however, had abnormal sperm. While he had plenty of sperm, none of them had tails; therefore, they couldn't swim. There was no way they were going to reach an egg. I sat in shock. After all the treatments I went through, not one doctor ever told us that Vinny should be checked out, *not one*! They just assumed it was me. I was furious. I felt like I had gone through years of treatment, enduring medications, and needles, being poked and prodded, all for nothing. I wasn't a lemon, after all. The good news was that the sperm's head—the part needed for fertilization—was healthy, so there shouldn't be a problem once we harvest the eggs. We had the green light, and even though my chances of conception weren't the highest, we had to try. We couldn't let this opportunity pass. We had to know that we did everything possible to have a biological child for our peace of mind.

Round one began. I received my box of infertility medications and needles, and the nurse showed Vinny and me how to fill the needles and how to administer the medication. I had to administer the shots to myself as Vinny did not like needles and would often turn green at their sight and practically pass out. I also had to go into the doctor's office every few days for blood work and an ultrasound to monitor my follicles and eggs. As the eggs were maturing and getting close to retrieval,

CHAPTER 8

the ultrasounds were getting more and more painful. I was uncomfortably bloated and very anxious.

Finally, it was retrieval day. We drove down to Chicago to the surgical center where Dr. Andrews performed her surgeries. Dr. Andrews came and explained the procedure. She said, "Keep in mind that because of your advanced age, we may only get one or two eggs, or we may not get any." We said we understood. The nurse came in to place the line in my arm for the anesthesiologist to administer the anesthesia, and they wheeled me down to the operating room. Vinny stayed in the recovery room to wait for me. The anesthesiologist must not have administered enough anesthesia. During the procedure, I was awoken by a painful, cramping feeling in my pelvic region. I remember seeing the surgical team in their scrubs and a bright light. The anesthesiologist must have administered some more anesthesia because when I woke up the next time, I was in the recovery room, where Vinny was waiting for me.

Vinny asked me how I felt, and I told him I had woken up during the procedure, and it hurt like heck. He kissed me on the forehead, "I'm sorry, honey." Dr. Andrews arrived a short time later with a smile on her face and said to me, "You are quite fertile; we were able to retrieve fifteen eggs! I will fertilize the eggs, and we will see how many are viable for implantation in about a week." Vinny and I were thrilled! We were not expecting fifteen eggs! I had been secretly hoping for at least five or six. "The nurse from the office will call you in a week. If you have any viable embryos, you will return to the surgical center, and I will implant them. Go home and rest."

Vinny and I were beyond excited, fifteen eggs! The next week or so would be hard to get through. I was so anxious I couldn't sleep more than a couple of hours each night. I tried to read or watch a movie, but mostly I just sat there in the darkness, sometimes in the nursery, my mind racing with thoughts of how it would feel to be pregnant. Would the baby be a boy or a girl? How many would we have? I would be thrilled to have twins. My mind flooded with thoughts and anticipation. I waited anxiously for the phone call. I was still in pain for about a week after the egg retrieval, but it would be worth it in the end. I wanted this so badly. It had been a week since the egg retrieval, and I had not heard from the doctor's office. I sat on the couch with Pippy as I nervously dialed the phone number and waited for someone to answer while stroking Pippy's velvet ears.

"Hello, this is Dr. Andrews' nurse, Nancy. How may I help you today?"

"Hi, Nancy," my voice filled with excitement. "This is Jessica Fontana. I am calling to check on my next steps with my IVF treatment."

"Hi, Jessica. Hold on a moment while I go grab your chart."

"Okay."

"Jessica?"

"Yes, I'm still here."

"The reason you didn't get a phone call is that none of the embryos were viable. There are no embryos to be implanted. I'm sorry." Her voice was so kind at the other end while I was sobbing on my end. "If you would like to try again, just let us know."

"Okay," I managed to say through my tears and hung up the phone. I laid on the couch for the rest of the afternoon with Pippy by my side and cried until Vinny came home.

"None of the embryos were viable," I said to him. Vinny hugged me, kissing the top of my head.

"I'm sorry, honey, we can try again if you want." I nodded my head, yes.

"Do you want to try again, Vinny?"

"Of course, but I know the shots and the medications make you sore and uncomfortable. We will try as many times as you want."

CHAPTER 8

A month or two later, round two. I was a little more prepared this time around and not as anxious. The ultrasounds every few days seemed to be more painful this time around. I was more bloated and uncomfortable too. Finally, it was egg retrieval day. Dr. Andrews came into my room.

"We were able to harvest fifteen eggs last time, so this time it probably won't be as many."

"Ok, we understand, but it only takes one good one," I said.

The nurse came into the room to place the line for anesthesia. She was digging and digging and digging, first in my left arm, then my right arm. I immediately bruised while Vinny almost passed out from the sight of the needle being dug into my arm. She finally gave up and went to look for someone a little more skilled and came back with the anesthesiologist. I told the anesthesiologist, a different one than I had last time, "Please make sure I get enough this time. Last time, I woke up in the middle of the procedure." The next thing I knew, I woke up with Vinny holding my hand in recovery.

"The procedure is over, honey. We're just waiting for Dr. Andrews." The anesthesia must have hit me before I left the room. At least this time, I was asleep for the entire procedure.

Dr. Andrews came in with a big smile on her face. She said, "Last time we got fifteen eggs, this time we got twenty-one!" I was not expecting that. I thought she would say we got five or less. We were thrilled, and Vinny took me home to rest. Again, I had many sleepless nights filled with anxiety, hoping, and praying for a viable transplant. *Please, God, let us have a viable transplant.* This time they called me.

"Hi, Jessica?" Nurse Nancy said on the other side of the phone. "You have three embryos to be implanted." I was beyond excited and crying again from joy and, of course, hormones.

"Thank you, Nancy!" I couldn't wait for Vinny to get home to share the news!

As soon as Vinny came in the door, I blurted out, "Three! We have three embryos! Oh, could you imagine triplets or twins? Oh my gosh, I'm so excited, Vin!" With a big grin on his face, he grabbed me and hugged me. He couldn't wait to be a dad, and he would be a good one.

Implantation day soon arrived. We drove down to Chicago for our very early appointment. We were so excited we got there before the staff! I was all set to be wheeled into the operating room when Dr. Andrews came in. She informed us that there were three embryos a couple of days ago, but we were down to two this morning. She just checked, and now we only had one embryo. The other one didn't make it. "Do you want me to go ahead with the implantation, or do you want to freeze this one and wait for another cycle and hopefully have more embryos to implant?"

I looked at her and said, "We don't have enough money for another round of IVF; this is our one and only shot, so go ahead with the implantation." The porter wheeled me to the operating room. This time I was not entirely out. Dr. Andrews was telling me step-by-step what she was doing, although I don't remember what she said, except for the embryo was in the tube, and she was going to implant it. She implanted the embryo, and then she performed an ultrasound. Before I knew it, I was back in my room. A short time later, when I was fully awake, Dr. Andrews came in, handed us a picture of the ultrasound, and told us the next steps. I should know in about 14 days if the implantation took hold.

Then she asked, "Do you want to know the sex of the baby?"

I looked at Vinny, and he said, "It's up to you, I can know, or I can wait, whatever you want to do." I said, "I kind of want to know the sex of the baby." The anticipation would have killed me for sure if I had to wait four months to find out.

CHAPTER 8

Dr. Andrews asked one more time, "Are you sure?" Please be a girl. Please be a girl. Please be a girl, I repeatedly said in my mind.

"Yes," we said in unison.

"Congratulations, it's a girl." I screamed, "YES!" I wanted a girl so badly! "Oh my gosh, Vin, I can't believe we are having a little girl!"

On the way home, we stopped for lunch at a Greek restaurant; for some reason, Vinny had a taste for Greek food, so I agreed. I thought to myself; we better get in all our eating out before the baby gets here. At lunch, all we talked about was the baby. What are we going to name her? I liked the name Bethany, but he didn't. He liked plain names, but I wanted something different, something I thought was pretty but not too commonplace. We would have time to think about it.

We only told mom, Jason, and Vinny's parents that we were going through IVF treatments. I didn't want the family bombarding me with questions and asking if I was pregnant. I didn't need any added stress. Once again, I was not sleeping; my anxiety was extremely high; my mind was continually racing. I tried to watch movies to try and quiet my mind, but it didn't work. I also sat quietly in the lavender nursery, rocking in the chair, imagining what it would like to be sitting there feeding my baby girl and rocking her. Still, my anxiety wouldn't subside. Two weeks later, I went in for blood work and a pregnancy test. I hoped this would be the last of the poking and prodding, at least for a while. I anxiously waited for the phone call with the results of my tests. I had a picture of the ultrasound on the fridge with an arrow pointing to the implantation. That little blip was our little girl! I just knew I was pregnant; my breasts were already sore.

The phone rang. It was the doctor's office. Finally, I would hear the words I have been waiting for most of my life. Congratulations, you're pregnant! The voice on the line said, "Jessica?"

"Speaking," I replied.

"This is Dr. Andrews' nurse, Nancy. We have the results of your tests, and I'm sorry to say you are not pregnant."

Instantly tears were streaming down my cheeks. I know the nurse heard me crying. "Okay," I managed to say, disappointed and sobbing.

"Please call us if you would like to try again or if you need any grief counseling. We are here for you, whatever you need."

"Okay." I hung up the phone.

I was utterly devastated. I really thought I was pregnant. Still crying, I went to the bathroom to get a tissue and decided I had to go pee. When I wiped, there was blood on the toilet paper, the start of my period. Had I had this information five minutes sooner, I would have been prepared for the news from the nurse and perhaps not so devastated. I retreated to the bedroom, Pippy followed. The two of us curled up in bed together in the fetal position, me uncontrollably sobbing, Pippy licking my tears away. Vinny arrived home, calling out to us. Pippy jumped down from the bed and stood at the top of the stairs barking until Vinny came up. Vinny looked at me and didn't even have to ask. Vinny lifted Pippy back up onto the bed and then joined us. Pippy resumed his position in front of me, snuggling into my chest while Vinny spooned me, kissing my head and holding me close as I continued to cry. I could hear him crying too.

He said, with a lump in his throat, "I'm sorry, honey. Are you mad at me?"

"Why would I be mad at you?"

"Because I couldn't give you a baby."

"It's not your fault. It's just something that happens. It's nothing you did or had any control over. No, I'm not mad at you. I love you."

CHAPTER 8

Red Velvet Cake

Ingredients for the cake:

2 1/2 cups all-purpose flour
1 teaspoon baking soda
1 teaspoon cocoa
1 1/2 cups granulated sugar
2 eggs
1 1/2 cups canola oil
1 teaspoon white vinegar
2 tablespoons red food coloring
1 teaspoon vanilla
1 cup buttermilk

Ingredients for the cream cheese frosting:

2 sticks butter (room temperature)
1 8 oz package cream cheese (room temperature)
4 cups powdered sugar, sifted
1 teaspoon vanilla
1 cup chopped, lightly toasted pecans (optional)

Directions for the cake:

Preheat oven to 350 degrees. Grease and flour 3 (9-inch) round layer cake pans.

Sift flour, baking soda, and cocoa together. Beat sugar and eggs together in a large bowl.

In a separate bowl, mix together oil, vinegar, food coloring, and vanilla, add to the bowl of eggs and sugar and beat until combined.

Add flour mixture and the buttermilk to the wet mixture by alternating the buttermilk and the dry ingredients. Always start with the flour and end with the flour.

Pour batter into pans. Tap them on the counter to level out the batter and release air bubbles. Bake for 25 minutes or until a cake tester inserted near the middle comes out clean. Careful not to overbake, or your cake will be dry!

Cool pans on a wire rack for about 10 minutes before turning out of the pan. Cool completely.

Directions for the frosting:

Cream together the butter and cream cheese. Add sugar and beat until mixed, but not so much the frosting becomes loose; add vanilla. Add nuts (optional).

Frost between layers and top and sides of the cake.

Enjoy! Jessica

Chapter 9

Vinny's co-worker, Steve, and his wife were pregnant after their IVF procedure, while I was absolutely devastated after losing our baby girl. I was still sore from the procedure and now had to deal with Aunt Flo on top of everything else. For the next two months, I laid in bed or on the couch. I felt paralyzed, unable to do anything—didn't want to do anything—or see anyone; I was severely depressed. I stared blankly at the ceiling or out the window, painful thoughts running through my mind flooded with guilt. My anxiety had been so high, and I felt that's why I lost the baby. I didn't create a healthy internal environment for her to survive in, even though I wanted her very much. Then came the thoughts of the finality of it all. We would never, ever be able to have a biological child.

I decided to call Katherine. I wanted to check on her and see how she was doing after surgery and her chemo treatments. I also wanted to ask about Grace and the baby as she had never reached out to us.

"Hi, Katherine, how is everything going?"

"Hi, Jess. Everything is going well. I'm responding to treatment and feeling good. Thank you for the cards and flowers. They really cheered me up. How are you doing?"

"Well, we had our embryo implanted, and she just didn't take. I lost her. I've been too devastated to call. I know I should have called sooner, but I just couldn't."

"It's okay, Jessica. I completely understand. I'm sorry you lost the baby."

"Thanks. I hesitated, "I was just wondering if you are still in touch with Grace. She never contacted us."

"Yes, I've talked to her a couple of times. She finally told her parents about the baby, last week and they were very receptive, which she didn't expect. Jess, she is keeping the baby. I'm sorry. I should have called you sooner."

"It's okay." I lied. I was secretly hoping Grace would contact us. "I figured she was keeping the baby since she never reached out to us." I knew it was a long shot, but I was secretly hoping she would reach out to us. "Let's set up a time next week to meet, I'll bring you lunch, and we can catch up some more."

"Sure, that would be nice, Jessica. I finally have my appetite back."

"It's a date. I'll call you next week. Bye, Katherine."

"Bye, Jess."

After a few months, Vinny and I talked about getting a donor egg and using his sperm to fertilize it, and then finding a surrogate to carry the baby. I was a little uneasy about this. I felt a bit jealous that the baby would not biologically be mine and that someone else got to carry the baby. Again, it came down to money. Insurance didn't pay for any of it, and we certainly didn't have the money. We ultimately decided against egg donation and surrogacy. Why did it have to be so expensive, anyway? We had tried the adoption route, and that was a bust. That was it; we were never going to be parents. We were never going to be grandparents.

I remembered something my hairstylist, Lynne, and I discussed some time ago. We had been discussing abortion. I was expressing how I wished women who were contemplating abortion knew how many people were out there wanting to be parents but couldn't. Why didn't these women realize there were plenty of people who would love and cherish that child and give the child a good life? The child they were thinking

CHAPTER 9

of aborting didn't have a choice in the matter. They were not only ending that child's life but the life of that child's future children. Who knows who they would have become or what they would have contributed to this world. Lynne was adopted as an infant, and she told me how grateful she was to her birth mother, who decided to give her life. She had wonderful adoptive parents and a great upbringing. If her birth mother had decided not to have her, she would not be here. Lynne's children and grandchildren would not exist. God doesn't make mistakes. A child is a blessing and should not be killed because it is inconvenient or unplanned.

Every day I woke up and felt like I hadn't slept at all. All-day long, I felt like I was moving in slow motion, struggling to move at all, as if I was walking through tar. My entire body hurt. I didn't have any interest in my hobbies, seeing people, or going anywhere, and I was still out of work. I was mad that some people who hurt children were allowed to have them. How come I couldn't? It's not fair. I wouldn't harm a child. I have so much love to give. Why hadn't God blessed us with a child? I was angry for a long, long time – years and years. I was lost. Whatever faith I had was gone. I was barely going through the motions of daily life. How did I end up on the exact opposite end of where I thought I would be at this time in my life? I felt like I was in a hole and couldn't get out.

Upon waking one morning, I looked in the mirror and was horrified at my reflection. I had aged. Fine lines and wrinkles had appeared, dark circles under my eyes, and a blank expression. I couldn't even smile. I felt like I was in there, but lost deep, deep inside. I was an emotionless, empty shell of myself.

After two months of just going through the motions of everyday life, I was clinically depressed, even though I didn't realize it at the time. I didn't shower every day. I didn't put on my makeup. My attire was sloppy; I only wore sweatpants and tee-shirts. I didn't care anymore. I didn't know why I was here. I didn't have a purpose. All I ever wanted was to be a mom, and that dream was over. It would never come true. I didn't know what to do with my life. I felt like no one needed me. I felt unwanted, alone, and lost.

I finally worked up the energy to venture out to the grocery store. My hair was messy. I didn't bother to put on makeup. I wore sweats and a tee-shirt, uncharacteristic for me in public. I didn't even care if I ran into anyone I knew. I just didn't. Every aisle I walked down, I saw the same mom with her two kids, one little one in the cart seat, and then the cutest little girl with big blue eyes and her hair in pigtails wearing a pink tee-shirt that read, I'm the big sister. She was holding the side of the cart. There wasn't enough room for both of us to get down the snack aisle, and the mom roughly pulled the little girl and said, "Watch out, get out of the way." I said, "It's ok, she's fine," and I smiled at the little girl. In every single aisle, I saw the same woman yelling at her little girl. The little girl was holding onto her mom's shirt, and the mom said in a very irritated voice, "Stop touching me! Let go of my shirt! Get out of the way!" I mean, where was this little girl going to go? It didn't matter if she held the cart or held her mom's shirt; her mom still scolded her. It took every fiber of my being not to go off on the mom. I quickly grabbed my items from the aisle and got away from them. I know I'm not a mom, but geez, lady, chill out. Another young mom I encountered was swearing at her child, calling him a little shit; he was about two-years-old. I cringed. What is wrong with people? Words hurt. I gathered the rest of my groceries and high-tailed it out of the store. I was back in my big, empty, lonely house. I sat on the couch in silence, staring at the wall, eating potato chips and cookies, and petting Pippy.

Months later, I was still despondent. To help perk me up, we decided to rescue another Italian Greyhound puppy. Later that week, we made the trip to the Wisconsin Italian Greyhound Rescue and brought Pippy with us so he could pick out his new brother or sister. We let Pippy interact with

CHAPTER 9

the pups, and he took a liking to a little tan male. This little puppy was a happy boy and bounced around like Tigger from Winnie the Pooh. He was the one. We brought him home and named him Tigger.

The months continued to whiz by; I laid in bed, wrapped warm and cozy in my blankets like a cocoon. I didn't want to get up. I laid there, staring at the ceiling. I didn't even know how many hours I had slept or how many hours I had been awake, staring. Who was I? What happened to the girl who would wake up at 5 a.m. and have all her chores done before starting work, ready to seize the day, full of energy? I was still tired in the morning and unable to get out of bed, sometimes lying there until 10 or 11 a.m. I would manage to move myself to the couch and just sit there, again staring out the window or at the wall. I didn't care how I looked, and I avoided mirrors. The only things that comforted me were being wrapped in a blanket, stuffing my face with junk food, or holding my dogs in my lap. I felt lost, and I was not sure how to find my way back. I'm not sure I wanted to.

Vinny kept himself busy, working as much as possible, and decided to earn his master's degree online. I barely saw him. He came home from work, grabbed his dinner, and ate it in the office while studying late into the night. I think this was his way of dealing with the loss. If he couldn't give me a baby, he could provide us with a comfortable living. Unfortunately, I was in this depression for years. I wanted to give up. The little voice inside me, which was but a whisper now, told me to keep going, so I did.

I'm not sure what prompted it, but it was time to stop wallowing in my non-mom status. I decided to look for a job, one working outside of the home. I ended up taking a job in a retail store, which meant working weekends and holidays again. I took a position in the customer service department, which I actually liked. It was my chance to help people out who were probably having a somewhat crummy day because they had to return an item or need help with something. I enjoyed it, and I became somewhat of a workaholic. I was the one who didn't have any family commitments; therefore, I came in every time I was called into work on my day off to cover for someone who was sick. Some of my co-workers didn't like that. They thought I was brown-nosing, but I wasn't. I just didn't want to be in a big, somewhat empty house. I had forgotten how catty workplaces could be, especially the female-dominated ones. The only thing I didn't like about the job was all the pregnant co-workers and customers and the daily reminder that I was not a mom and never would be. My co-workers were always talking about their kids, a conversation I could not take part in, once again feeling like I didn't belong.

Being childless, not by choice, sucks. I would be going about my day just fine and dandy when WHAM! Something completely innocent and unexpected triggered me. On this particular day, it was a trip to the department store to buy a new sweater for Christmas. I walked into the store, and the first thing I saw was a display of a mannequin family dressed in matching buffalo checked pajamas. We were going to be one of those families. I started to daydream. We would dress in matching pajamas on Christmas Day, watching the joy on our children's faces as they ripped open their gifts. Then later eating breakfast--eggs, bacon, and pancakes—watching the children play with their new games and toys, getting along with each other, and having fun. But Vin and I barely celebrated Christmas anymore. Some Christmases, I didn't even put up a tree, and if I did, I didn't decorate it. Vinny and I didn't exchange gifts because we bought whatever we wanted throughout the year. We saw the family on Christmas Eve, but we were usually home alone, relaxing and watching movies by the fireplace with the pups on Christmas Day. It wasn't always like this. When we were first married, I enjoyed putting up the tree and decorating the house. I did a ton of baking, and I enjoyed it. But, somewhere along the way, Christmas became

CHAPTER 9

a chore, and it wasn't enjoyable anymore. I almost stopped participating altogether.

*　*　*

I picked out a sweater and browsed the store for Christmas gifts. I decided to buy the red and black buffalo checked pajamas for our youngest niece and nephew and toys to donate to Toys for Tots. I waited in the check-out line. When it was my turn, I was greeted by a thirty-something woman who started to make small talk as she rang up my items.

"These pajamas are cute. I bought a set for my boys; she said as she folded them and placed them in the bag. How many children do you have?"

"I'm childless due to health issues," I replied.

"That will be $162.78," she said. I swiped my credit card. "You're lucky your husband didn't leave you," she said as she handed me the bag. I instantly flashed back to my childhood when my bully Kimmy walloped me in the face with a ball during a game of dodgeball so hard that it knocked me off my feet, and it stung. The cashier's words that seemingly came out of nowhere administered the same jolt and pierced my core. I was stunned as her cruel words rang in my ears. I grabbed my bag, hung my head so no one could see the tears filling my eyes. I left the store, walking as fast as my chubby legs could carry me to my car. I sat in my vehicle in shock, desperately searching my purse for a tissue to wipe the tears away. It's not me with health issues. I cannot believe people don't think before they speak! I wanted to go into the store and talk to her manager, but instead, I headed home, abandoning the rest of my chores for the day. It was only 10 a.m., and with one quip of the tongue, she had ruined my day. Unfortunately, comments like these were an almost daily occurrence. Flashbacks of my childhood raced through my mind. I was in a game of dodgeball all over again, and I was an unwilling participant.

I needed to call my person, Katherine. She would understand and know exactly what to say to make me feel better.

As the months went on, everywhere I went was a constant reminder of what I didn't have. Families everywhere enjoying their time together at the park, in the store, eating out, excited about upcoming holidays. The 4th of July was coming up, and I was falling into an even deeper depression. Our baby girl had been due around the 4th of July, so this holiday would forever be a reminder of the baby we lost. I was so looking forward to it, too. I would have baked her a red, white, and blue birthday cake for her every year. The whole family would gather at our home for a barbecue to celebrate our baby girl's birthday and our country's birthday, too. It would have been so much fun. Now I just hid in my house with Vin and the pups. We watch the fireworks inside through our patio door, as not to scare the dogs. Our house faces the golf course where our town sets off fireworks; it's perfect.

CHAPTER 9

Brownie Biscotti

Ingredients:

1/2 cup butter, melted
3 eggs
2 teaspoons vanilla extract
2-1/2 cups all-purpose flour
1-1/3 cups sugar
3/4 cup baking cocoa
2 teaspoons baking powder
1/2 teaspoon baking soda
1 cup toasted sliced almonds, toasted
1/2 cup miniature semisweet chocolate chips

Directions:

In a large bowl, combine the butter, eggs, and vanilla mix well. Combine the flour, sugar, cocoa, baking powder, and baking soda and gradually add to the butter mixture; just until combined, the dough will be crumbly.

Turn dough out onto a lightly floured surface, knead in almonds and chocolate chips. Divide dough in half. On an ungreased baking sheet, shape each portion into a 12" x 3" log, leaving 3" in between the logs.

Bake at 325 degrees for 30-35 minutes or until set and tops are cracked. Cool for 15 minutes. Transfer to cutting board. Cut diagonally with a serrated knife into 1/2 inch slices. Place cut side down on ungreased baking sheets—Bake for 20-25 minutes or until firm and dry. Move to wire racks to cool.

Drizzle with melted chocolate if desired.

Enjoy! Jessica

Chapter 10

I started ruminating about how I've spent most of my life grieving in secret, always on the outside looking in. As a child, I was shy, and I was picked on relentlessly by my classmates. I never knew why they picked on me. All I ever wanted was to be accepted by my peers. As an adult, I am a member of a club that I never asked to join. I never thought in a million years; I would be a part of a grieving, misunderstood community. We are a secret society that suffers in silence. We are *childless, not by choice.*

Every single day from the moment I wake up in the morning to the moment I go to bed, I'm in an unsolicited game of dodgeball. There is no protective equipment in dodgeball, no helmet, no pads, just a ball. From the moment I step out of my house, I'm on guard. I never know when I'm going to get hit with an emotional zinger. In the past, I could avoid the game by not leaving the house, but now the game is in my house, on social media. At least in my house, I can choose not to participate most of the time.

Most days, my game of dodgeball starts full swing at work. My co-workers talk about their weekend, spending time with their kids doing this and that. Occasionally, I get walloped by yet another co-worker who is pregnant. For the next nine months, I'll have to watch as her belly grows, there is talk about a baby shower, and hear baby names thrown around. I pretend it doesn't bother me, even though it hurts immensely. I smile. I'm polite. I am genuinely happy for her but secretly

CHAPTER 10

hoping I don't receive an invitation to the baby shower. I'm already formulating a plan to *be busy* that day. If the baby shower is for a family member or close friend, of course, I will be there, but if it's for a co-worker or someone I don't know really well, I'd rather skip it. I'd rather avoid the question, *do you have children*? I'd say no, and the conversation would turn awkward or stop altogether, and then I would become invisible to the other guests, anyway. No thanks. Hard pass.

The game of dodgeball is especially tricky when running errands. It doesn't matter what store I'm in. A woman is toting a child. Sometimes the child is crying and screaming and carrying on, and the mother seems oblivious. Some are acting out and pushing all the "mom buttons." Some are just so freaking adorable I can't stand it, and my heartaches. I have to pretend it doesn't bother me, but it does. I have to give that fake smile—you know the one—that forced smile where you don't show your teeth, appearing to understand what it's like to be a mom when I'm feeling especially vulnerable in reality. I shop on the off-hours just to avoid these situations as much as possible.

On other days, I play the game of dodgeball in my house. I avoid watching commercials on TV. I avoid social media many days, especially those days when it's Daughter's Day, Son's Day, Grandparent's Day, or the first day of school. Those get to me.

The holidays are the worst for dodgeball, as I'm at my most vulnerable. I'm getting bombarded at every angle. I have to pretend that I am happy when, most of the time, I'm not. I am continually thinking of how my child would be interacting with family members, opening her gifts, the photo opportunities, the memories we would have created and shared. In a room full of family, I don't have much to say. I'm more of an observer, not a participator. I'm invisible. They are full of joy, and I am full of pain. I keep it hidden with an Oscar-worthy performance. At the end of the day and the end of the dodgeball game, I'm tired and worn out, emotionally battered and bruised. When I get home, I will relax a bit before going to bed, for tomorrow is another day—another game of dodgeball—and I don't even know who my opponents are going to be.

CHAPTER 10

Honey Icebox Cookies

Ingredients:

1 1/2 cups shortening
2 cups packed brown sugar
2 eggs
1/2 cup honey
1 teaspoon lemon extract
4 1/2 cups all-purpose flour
2 teaspoons baking soda
2 teaspoons baking powder
1 teaspoon salt
1 teaspoon ground cinnamon.

Directions:

- In a large bowl, cream shortening and brown sugar until fluffy. Add eggs one at a time beating well after each one. Beat in honey and lemon extract. Combine the remaining ingredients and gradually add to the creamed mixture and mix well.

- Shape into two 12-inch rolls, wrap each roll in plastic wrap. Refrigerate 2 hours or until firm.

- Unwrap and cut into 1/4 inch slices. Place 1 inch apart on an ungreased baking sheet. Bake at 325 degrees for 12-14 minutes or until golden brown. Cool slightly and move to a wire rack to cool completely.

Enjoy! Jessica

Chapter 11

I was enjoying my job and decided it was time to venture outside of my comfort zone. I enrolled in a local cake decorating school. I enjoyed it, and I was good at it. It was a six-month-long, part-time course, and my employer was kind enough to work around my class schedule. The class was once a week, and we had the rest of the week to practice what we just learned. My neighbors were happy because I gave them all my practice cakes. I practiced writing with icing and perfecting icing borders and flowers in my spare time, and I loved it. I gained an appreciation for all the time and creativity it took to make a beautiful cake that tasted great too. The only thing I didn't like was that my masterpiece was eaten in ten minutes!

I met many nice women in my class, including a couple of young women who had toddlers and a few older women like myself who, of course, always talked about their grandchildren and how they couldn't wait to make cakes for their birthdays. *Ugh.* I must have heard a thousand times that being a grandma is the best job in the world or having grandchildren is the best thing ever to happen to me. Once again, I was an outsider. I didn't have any stories to share about children or grandchildren. I nodded my head and pretended I understood.

I learned many tips and tricks of the trade during the cake decorating course, adding to my baking knowledge. The months seemed to fly by, and it was final exam day. It was time to show the instructor that we had mastered our piping and

CHAPTER 11

flower-making skills using different frostings—buttercream, whipped cream, and fondant. We baked our cakes at home for the final exam and decorated them at school as our grade was dependent on our decorating skills and technique. I had arranged with Mindi to take me to the class that day as my car was in the shop for repairs. My creative side was peeking out, and Mindi hated it. I think she would have liked me to stay unfulfilled, depressed, and miserable. I called Mindi that morning. "Hi Mindi, I just wanted to remind you to please be on time picking me up today. This is my final exam, and I'm going to need every minute."

"Of course! I will be there to drive you and your cakes to school." She actually sounded happy for me.

I told Vinny of the plan. "If you need me, call me. I'll pick you up and drive you to school," he said.

"Okay," I replied. "Mindi promised she would drive me." He rolled his eyes, knowing that she had disappointed me many, many times before with no explanation or even acknowledgment that she didn't do what she said she was going to do. I fell for it *every single time.*

Three-thirty rolled around, and no Mindi. I called her phone and got her voicemail, and left a message. "Hey Mindi, it's Jessica, its 3:30 pm, and I hope you are on your way. Call me if there is a problem." I called a couple more times left messages for Mindi. She was not picking up the phone, nor was she at my house to drive me to school; it was now 3:45 pm. I called Vin. I didn't have to say anything.

"Already on my way, honey, I'm almost there. I knew she would do this to you." He always had my back. He arrived a couple of minutes later. He helped me load my cakes into the car and drove me and my cakes to school with no time to spare.

I was frazzled and not as calm as I had wanted to be. I was rushing to gather my tools and ingredients to prep my station so I could frost and decorate my cakes. *Damn Mindi.* I thought something had happened to her. I thought she got into an accident or something. Nope, she just blew me off. She never acknowledged that she didn't show up that day or that she had let me down. To this day, I know she did it on purpose because she didn't want me to succeed. I don't know why, but I never called her on it. I guess I didn't want to hear another one of her lame excuses. I needed to get away from toxic people, and Mindi was definitely one of those people, even if she was family.

I made a couple of mistakes during my exam, but I told the instructor I knew what I did wrong, and only half-points were deducted. I passed my final exam with flying colors. My cake was delicious. Any area I made a mistake, I covered it with a flower. I had completed the course successfully, and I received my certificate.

Although I had made cakes and cookies for family parties and some friends, now I was able to wow them with my decorating skills as well. Three months after finishing the cake decorating school, I started a small decorated cake side business, more of a hobby. I only made cakes for family and friends that I knew. My county did not allow home kitchens to be licensed. I had to rent out a place to bake if I wanted to be a legitimate company. I spoke to a lawyer, and he told me I could not have a "real business," but it was okay to charge money to family and friends for baked goods. I was okay with that. I was making a little pocket money and doing something I enjoyed. Within two years, my cake business was taking off; I had a loyal following. I was ready to start looking for a place to open a small bakery.

One day, Vinny came home with news that the company he worked for was sold to one of their clients. His new employer was located in Wisconsin. Vinny had been commuting two days a week to this client's office in Wisconsin for over a year, and it was taking a toll on him. He was crabby and tired all the time, and he seemed to get sick a lot and had had a bout of walking pneumonia. I was distraught at the prospect of

CHAPTER 11

having to move. I thought I would die in this house; I'm emotionally attached to it. We picked out all the exterior and interior details, from the brick's color and siding to the lighting, the tile, and the paint colors. We personalized this home. We loved our home and our neighborhood. This was *our* home, even if it was just the two of us and Pippy and Tigger. I was conflicted, I didn't *want* to move, but at the same time, this could be a fresh start somewhere new. The bigger picture, though, this was an excellent opportunity for Vinny.

I stopped taking cake and cookie orders as I could not commit to completing them, and we started house hunting. We also started getting our home ready to be put on the market. I staged it as if an actual family with children lived there. It took us the entire summer looking for homes closer to Wisconsin before we decided on one. We purchased a ranch house in Lily Lake, a lake and golf course community out in the country, close to the Illinois/ Wisconsin border.

We sold our home quickly to a newly married young couple. They were practically getting a new home as the three upstairs kids' bedrooms and bathroom were never used. We had a huge garage sale. I was finally coming to terms that we were never going to be parents, and I sold the crib and rocker recliner as well as the ducky bathroom accessories. We were set to move Labor Day weekend. I broke my mom's rule once again, now living an hour and a half away. She was not too happy about that.

Betty's Brownies

Ingredients:

1 cup butter, melted and cooled
3 eggs
1-1/2 teaspoon vanilla extract
1 cup all-purpose flour
1 cup sugar
1 cup packed brown sugar
3/4 cup baking cocoa
1-1/2 teaspoon baking powder

Icing:

1/2 cup butter, softened
1-1/4 cups confectioners' sugar
2/3 cup baking cocoa
2 tablespoons milk
2 tablespoons hot brewed coffee
1 teaspoon vanilla extract

Directions:

In a large bowl, combine the butter, eggs, and vanilla. Combine the dry ingredients, gradually add to the butter mixture. Do not overmix

Spread into greased 13"x 9" baking pan. Bake at 350 degrees for 25-30 minutes or until a toothpick inserted in the middle comes out clean. Cool in pan on a wire rack.

Combined icing ingredients in a small bowl, beat until smooth. Spread over the cooled brownies. Cut into bars.

Enjoy! Jessica

Chapter 12

Our move out to the country was an adjustment. Country living is slow-paced, relaxing, and the people were friendly. The air was fresh; it somehow seemed cleaner and smelled sweeter than back in the suburbs. There were stands on the side of the road with fresh vegetables, fruits, and eggs, most of which had a little tin box to put your money in, whatever amount you felt was fair for what fresh foods you are taking. I saw cows, horses, chickens, pheasants, and turkeys regularly. I found it weird, driving down the street and having to stop so a turkey could cross the road. I encounter large farming machinery; I can't imagine its use, but it would crush my car if I got in its way--these are everyday occurrences.

Not many people knew about our little subdivision, tucked away, surrounded by farmland, and not at all visible from the main highway. Most folks live here year-round, while others come out from Chicago on weekends and holidays to relax and get away from the city's hustle and bustle. Nevertheless, it's relatively peaceful out in the country, although a little too quiet for my liking. We've met a few neighbors, and they call me city girl, although I'm far from it, more of a suburban girl. I liked the convenience of being close to stores, restaurants, and doctors. I felt quite unsettled, not having my pick of several craft stores within minutes from each other. I now drove forty minutes one way to get to a craft store, big-box store, or restaurant. Our new town only had one stoplight in a major intersection off the main highway. Only one small grocery store served as the hardware store, dry cleaner, and movie rental place.

That first winter had been long and snowy, and by the middle of spring, I was still searching for a job. I hadn't baked since moving here, not even Christmas cookies. I was feeling very isolated.

I was on my way to establish myself and Vinny with a primary care doctor, Dr. Murphy. He was fresh out of medical school and had joined an established medical practice. I arrived at the urgent care center where Dr. Murphy had office hours a couple of days a week, the other days, and he was at the big hospital seeing patients there. It was immaculate and well-staffed. I checked in and took my seat in the packed waiting room. There were babies and small children. Some were crying, some were coughing, and some were wiping runny noses on their sleeves. *Yuck.* There were quite a few adults, mostly farm people reading agriculture magazines or watching Maury Povich on TV. Others sat in silence like me. It didn't take long, and the nurse called my name, "Jessica?" I stood up and followed the nurse. The first stop was the dreaded scale. I was overweight, and I'm sure the doctor would give me the same spiel, eat less, eat healthy foods, and exercise more, blah, blah, blah. Like I hadn't tried all of that before. The nurse took me into the exam room and started with her questioning.

"What brings you in today?" she inquired.

"My husband and I just moved here. We are looking for a primary care physician, and Dr. Murphy was on our plan. I need my annual physical."

The nurse took my temperature and blood pressure.

"Are you taking any medications?"

"No, just vitamin supplements and ibuprofen when needed."

"What vitamins are you taking?"

"Vitamin D3, Krill oil, calcium, iron, and vitamin C."

CHAPTER 12

"On a scale of one to ten, with ten being the saddest and one being the happiest, where would you say you are today?"

I never had that question before and thought about it for a second. I found this question peculiar but answered it honestly. "I'm about eight." She wrote that in her notes.

"The doctor will be in to see you shortly."

"Thank you."

I was a little cold and wished I had worn a long-sleeved shirt. I always seemed to be cold. I heard a knock on the door.

"Come in," I said.

"Hi, Jessica?"

"Yes."

"I'm Dr. Murphy, and I will be taking care of you today."

Dr. Murphy was very tall, with straight brown hair, boyish-looking. He asked again why I was there, and I told him that I was there to establish him as our primary care physician and just have a check-up. He looked in my ears, my throat, listened to my heart, had me lay back, and felt around my abdomen.

As I sat up, he looked me in the eye and said, concernedly, "I see you are feeling sad today. Eight is quite high. Why are you feeling so sad, Jessica?" No one had ever asked me that before. I thought about it briefly.

"My husband and I just moved here. I had to leave my family and friends." I was overcome by emotions and tried to hold back the tears. "I don't know anyone here, and I'm not working." By the time I finished my sentence, I had tears running down my face.

"I see. Anything else?"

"Yes." I hesitated and sighed. "We lost our daughter. I went through IVF infertility treatments, and she just didn't take. I don't know if that is considered a miscarriage or not." I had never actually said those words out loud to anyone before, and it made me start crying even harder. Dr. Murphy handed me some tissues.

"I'm sorry, Jessica. Did you seek any counseling after the loss of the baby?"

"No."

"Is there anything else I should know? Anything else you want to tell me?"

I added, "For the past few months, I haven't enjoyed my hobbies, baking and paper crafting. I haven't paper crafted for a year or so, and I'm not feeling inspired. I used to enjoy those things."

"Jessica, I think you would benefit from seeing a psychiatrist. I think you may be suffering from depression, and you need some help and possibly medication."

I was dumbfounded. I didn't know what to say except "okay." I felt some relief and some fear as I didn't want people to think I was crazy. As in many families, our family did not talk about feelings, and there was a stigma attached to mental illness. Before I left, Dr. Murphy wrote on his prescription pad that I should paper-craft at least three times a week to awaken my creative side and to feel more engaged with life. He also sent me home with a list of psychiatrists' who took my insurance. I agreed to call one of them as soon as possible and make an appointment. I went home and cried the rest of the day, feeling somewhat relieved, and told Vinny what was going on.

"You haven't seemed yourself in a while," Vin said to me. "You seem irritable and short-tempered and easily agitated. I thought it was because of the move. We left a house you loved, and you don't know anyone here. Not to mention, you are not working." Vin was always supportive and never criticized how I dealt with losing the baby, even when I put weight back on due to stress eating and laid in bed all day. He let me work through my feelings on my own. I hadn't realized my irritability and felt horrible that I may have snapped at him without merit. I wished he had spoken up sooner and brought this to my attention.

CHAPTER 12

"I've never really had a lot of time where I wasn't working. It's given me time to think, the childhood bullying, losing my gram and dad, the failed adoption and IVF, the loss of our baby girl, and now moving away from our family and friends. All the emotions I've suppressed over the years have come to a boiling point, and I don't know how to handle it. I've shut down. I'm completely out of my comfort zone and feeling lost."

"I think talking to someone would be helpful, honey."

I called to make an appointment with Dr. Emmerson. I preferred a female doctor. If I was going to be baring my soul, talking about my failure to become a mother, I didn't want to do that with a male psychiatrist. She was able to see me in a week.

I arrived at the office and weaved by through the men standing outside smoking to get to the door. I hated the smell of cigarette smoke; it brought up unpleasant thoughts of my dad's cancer as it was caused by smoking. The building on the inside looked like something from the 1970s, and it needed a makeover. The walls were orange and avocado green. The furniture was drab with flowery patterns and was not at all comfortable.

The walls adorned with weird-looking paintings of waiflike girls with big eyes and snakes coming out of their heads, interesting choice for a psychiatrist's office, I thought to myself. I signed in and waited for the nurse to call my name. I wondered what everyone was doing there, as I'm sure they were thinking the same of me. Most of the people in the waiting room looked disheveled. I didn't know if it was because they were lazy, down and out, or just didn't care. Some looked like they had just gotten out of bed. Some looked sad, tired, and beaten down. Some were even filthy. It was as if they didn't care how they seemed to others, unlike me.

I could have come to the doctor's office unkempt, looking like I did at home lately. I chose to look put-together. My hair was pretty, I had makeup on, and I was clean; this was just another way I kept my grief a secret. I pretended I was happy and in control when, in reality, I was biting my nails, and my trichotillomania had resurfaced for the first time since my twenties. I was a ball of stress and anxiety. I wondered how I looked to them; was I fooling them? The nurse called my name. I stood up and followed her. She took my weight, temperature, and blood pressure and proceeded to take me to Dr. Emmerson's office.

I walked into the office, and there was my psychiatrist, Dr. Emily Emmerson. She stood about five-foot-three-inches, with short dark hair, flawless pale skin, and big brown eyes. She was nicely dressed. She was plain and soft-spoken.

"Hi Jessica, I'm Dr. Emmerson. It's nice to meet you," she extended her hand.

"Hi." I gave a small nervous smile and shook her hand.

"Have a seat, Jessica. Let's get to know each other."

"Okay." I sat down on the couch, which, to my surprise, was quite comfortable. I put my purse next to me, grabbed a pillow, and placed it on my lap, hugging it close to my abdomen. I didn't know what to say. "Where do you want me to start?"

"How about from the point where you started feeling sad, Jessica."

"Okay."

I thought to myself; this is going to take a long time. She's going to make a lot of money off of me.

CHAPTER 12

Pumpkin Sheet Cake

Ingredients Pumpkin Sheet Cake:

1 cup (2 sticks) butter, melted
1 cup whole milk
1/2 cup pureed plain pumpkin (canned)
2 cups granulated sugar
2 large eggs
1 teaspoon vanilla extract
2 cups flour
1 teaspoon baking soda
1 teaspoon pumpkin pie spice
1/2 teaspoon salt

Cinnamon Cream Cheese Frosting:

1/2 cup (1 stick) butter
8 oz cream cheese
1/3 cup whole milk
1 teaspoon vanilla extract
1 teaspoon cinnamon
5 1/2 cups powdered sugar

Directions for the sheet cake:

Preheat oven to 350 degrees. Grease a 13 x 18 jelly roll pan with butter or Pam cooking spray.

In a large bowl, whisk together melted butter, milk, pumpkin, and sugar. Whisk in eggs and vanilla extract. Then whisk in flour, baking soda, pumpkin pie spice, and salt.

Pour batter into prepared jelly roll pan and bake for 20 minutes or until a toothpick inserted in the center comes out clean.

Directions for the cream cheese frosting:

In a large bowl, cream the butter and cream cheese until smooth. At low speed, beat in milk, vanilla extract, and cinnamon until combined. Whisk in the powdered sugar, beating on high until frosting is smooth. Spread the frosting on top of the cooled cake.

Refrigerate cake until ready to serve. Let cake sit on the counter for 10 minutes before serving.

Enjoy! Jessica

Chapter 13

We started meeting our neighbors as it was getting warmer and more people were outside. Vin and I decided to participate in the community garage sale. It was quite a big deal for our little town. It was called Treasures by the Lake, and hundreds of people came from all over. It was so popular; in fact, the home owner's association provided maps of the participating homes and items they were selling. They set up an area where food trucks could park and serve their food, and the HOA also rented Port-A-Potty's.

We were greeted by several of our neighbors throughout the day, welcoming us to the neighborhood, and we chatted a bit. Most everyone we lived by was around our age, mid-forties or older, as this subdivision was supposed to be a fifty-five and over community. With the 2008 housing crisis, the developer went bankrupt, and now the lots are sold to anyone regardless of age. There was a mix of younger couples and older couples. It was a very active community. There were always people walking around or driving around in their golf carts and activities at the clubhouse.

We met our neighbors Janet and Ian, who lived across the street and down a couple of houses. Ian introduced himself and his wife and asked us the dreaded question, "How many children do you have?"

"We don't have any. Not by choice, we were unable to have children." I said.

"If you are ever interested in fostering, let me know. I work for the state in the foster care system. This area needs more foster parents."

"We never gave it any thought. We don't know anything about being a foster parent."

"Well, if you ever think it's something you would want to do, let me know, and I can come over and explain to you how it works."

"Ok, we'll think about it."

"Great! Nice to meet you, folks. I'm sure we will see you around the neighborhood."

"Nice to meet you too, take care."

Later that evening, Vin and I talked about foster care. We decided we should hear Ian out. We hadn't thought of fostering, and we didn't know all that much about it. The next time we saw Ian or Janet, we would invite them over.

A week or so later, we invited Ian and Janet over to talk about potentially fostering.

"Hi guys, welcome to our home," I said. "May I get either of you an iced tea or water?"

"Iced tea sounds great," said Janet. "Make that two," Ian chimed in.

"Coming right up." "Vin, you want anything?"

"Nah, I'm good, honey."

Vin ushered them out onto our big beautiful deck overlooking the golf course. We had just purchased some new deck furniture, and Vin was dying to break it in. I gathered the beverages and joined them. We started talking about potentially fostering. Ian reiterated the need for foster parents in our area. He went over the classes we would have to take and told us we would have to have our home inspected and approved and a few other things. Then he said to us, "the goal of being a foster parent is to provide a stable environment for the child, but ultimately we would like the child to be able to go back to their biological parents if possible." He gave us

CHAPTER 13

Sarah's phone number; she was in charge of setting up the classes and the home study and could answer any additional questions we had.

Vin and I thought about it for several weeks. We called Sarah with all of our questions, and she was gracious enough to answer each one of them. While sympathetic, and we saw the need, it just wasn't for us. We didn't feel we could foster a child and then send them back to their biological parents. We knew we would get too attached. Fostering was out of the question. Later, Ian told us about an adoption agency that had a high success rate of placement. Friends of theirs adopted a baby after only five months. We decided to check it out.

We went to Warm Hugs Adoption Agency and sat through the orientation. They only had one spot left. We decided to try and get in; what did we have to lose? The next day, Debbie, one of the agency owners, called us to set up an interview. The adoption agency was an hour and a half drive from us, and Vin took a day off work. I still wasn't working at this time, and off we went to the interview.

Debbie could not have been sweeter. She went over the process with us and answered all our questions. She went over the fee. They required half up-front, twenty-thousand dollars, and the other half if adoption were to take place. I didn't know where we would get the money, but we would figure it out. I hoped that we were finally going to get our baby; we just needed to wait for Debbie's phone call.

Debbie called the very next day to welcome us into the program! We were thrilled! We had one week to write them a check or charge the fee to our credit card. This is getting real, I thought to myself. We also had a lot of homework to do. We had to put together an online profile with pictures. It was tough to write to a potential birthmother and explain why we would be the best choice for her baby, as this would be a very emotional and permanent decision for her. We had to meet with our caseworker for a home study, take a bunch of classes, and undergo a background check. We had to be finger-printed, submit financial records, take a CPR class, and read a few books. *Whew!* It was quite invasive, but we had nothing to hide. I had not so much as a speeding ticket since I was eighteen. We were good people, and we knew we would be great parents. We just needed a birthmother to see that too and choose us. We were excited and scared all at the same time. I wondered if my therapy would be an issue.

Angie, our caseworker, was sweet. She took the time to answer all our questions and discuss anything we wanted but never promised us anything. She said, "you never know what is going to trigger a birthmother's choice. It could be a picture in your profile that reminds her of her childhood; someone in one of your photographs could resemble someone in her family or the things you enjoy doing she enjoys too." We included pictures with our parents, siblings and nieces and nephews, and family gatherings such as Christmas and game night. Photos of me in my craft room and baking and Vin on the golf course, pictures of our pups, and our subdivision at the lake, beach, and surrounding area. Our bio included that we lived in the Midwest in a golf and lake community, our hobbies, and things Vinny and I enjoyed doing together. Vin and I were diligent about getting everything done that we needed to; all our ducks were in a row. Now we had to sit and play the waiting game and pray, pray, pray.

In the beginning, we only told a few people about the adoption—Vin's parents, my mom, Jason, and my friend Katherine. I started looking at nursery items. I felt positive it was going to be a girl and only shopped for girl items. I went to a baby store and spoke with a retail associate there. I announced proudly that my husband and I were in the process of adopting a baby. She congratulated me and gave me a checklist of all the baby items we would need. If I wanted to set up a registry to let her know, she also gave me a welcome bag with newborn diapers, a bottle, baby wash and lotion,

CHAPTER 13

and lots of coupons. I told her we were just in the beginning process of the adoption. I didn't want to register just yet, not until a birthmother chose us. I walked around the store looking at all the cute items, and within fifteen minutes, I was utterly overwhelmed with everything this tiny human would need. There were so many gadgets to make life easier for baby and parents, and *wow*, everything was expensive, super cute, and I wanted it all!

I arrived home from the baby store and told Vinny about all the baby items we would need.

"I don't want you buying one baby item until a birthmother officially chooses us. Remember, there are no guarantees." Vin said.

"I know you are right, but everything is so cute, I don't know if I can resist. Besides, I have a good feeling about this Vin. This adoption agency has a high placement rate. We've waited so long I just know we will be chosen. I can feel it."

It was a tough task. I'm a planner, and I wanted to be ready and organized. I was excited, and at my next therapy session, I told Dr. Emmerson the news. I asked if she thought my therapy would be an issue. She said no, it shouldn't be an issue. There were many people in therapy, and I was making good progress.

Christmas was arriving, and it was our turn to host Vin's family. We would tell his brother and sister, nieces and nephews about the adoption on Christmas. I was finally going to be able to make my birth announcement the way I had always planned—pink and blue balloons in a big plastic storage tote that floated up when the tote was opened. I was so excited and filled with hope that this would be our last *childless* Christmas.

Vin's family filled our home on Christmas Day. We played games and ate way too much. After dinner, the women cleaned the kitchen and brought out all of the desserts. The men helped arrange the furniture, so we were all sitting in a circle. The kids sorted the presents and made piles next to everyone's seat. Finally, it was time to open presents. We watched as our nieces and nephews opened all their gifts, and then the adults. I was on the edge of my seat the entire time; I could barely contain my excitement! Finally, we finished with the gift opening, and Vin announced that we had one more gift, and this one, in a way, was for the whole family. Everyone was intrigued. Vin went into the spare room, brought out the big blue storage tote, and placed it in front of his parents. "Gramma and Papa, will you do the honor of opening this one last present for everyone?" Vin's mom opened the lid, and the balloons floated out. At first, there was no reaction. Then, my sister-in-law, Gina, started to cry, and she hugged me. Vin stepped in and said, "Now, before you get all excited, we are not pregnant, but we have signed with an adoption agency." Everyone seemed to be happy for us and had lots of questions. I brought out our adoption profile to show everyone. I said, "We have not been chosen yet, but this adoption agency has a high placement rate, and we are staying positive. We would appreciate it if everyone would pray for us to finally make our family complete." Vin and I then took a picture by the Christmas tree holding the pink and blue balloons and the Mylar balloon with the word "baby" on it. I could not wait to put this picture in my scrapbook!

We went to see my family the next weekend to celebrate Christmas. I brought our adoption profile with me and showed it to my mom, who already knew of our plan, and Jason. I had not told Mindi and was not sure how she would react. She didn't say much except, "do we still throw a baby shower for you?" I was not quite sure what to say to her and not sure why she said that. Wouldn't she accept our baby as part of the family? Would she make him or her feel different? I said, "I don't see why not. A baby still needs a good start in life." My mom chimed in, "Of course, we will have a baby shower. It's to celebrate and welcome a new member of our family."

CHAPTER 13

Every time the phone rang, we held our breath and hoped it was the phone call we had been anticipating. We received our phone call every month from the adoption agency with the same spiel. "Your profile has been viewed many times. There just has not been a match yet." When we went to the adoption agency's online webpage, we could see our profile and others, and we could see that people had been viewing our profile a lot. Vin and I were sure a birthmother would choose us. We were staying positive. As the months went on, no one in the family really asked us if there was any interest in our profile, except my mom.

Vin and I were still excited and did not give up hope. I didn't know if our family thought we were making a mistake; maybe they thought we were too old. We were forty-five now. Perhaps they simply didn't want to pry. We didn't talk about it unless someone else brought it up, and they hardly brought it up. I once again prayed to God; *please give us a baby. We would be such great parents.* I talked to Katherine often. She called to see how I was doing and if anyone had chosen us yet. "Not yet," I would tell her month after month, still hopeful. She always knew just what to say to comfort me. She was my only friend who was childless, not by choice; she understood the pain. She was my person. I missed not living closer to her. We talked on the phone at least once a week.

We continued to wait for our phone call, anticipating that any day could be the day a birthmother chose us. We had our regular home visits with our social worker Angie, and we had a long list of names picked out. We heard another couple in our group had adopted twin boys; we were so excited for them. We were still hopeful a birthmother would choose us and sad at the same time that we had not been chosen yet. Why wasn't anyone picking us? My anxiety started to creep in, and my trichotillomania and nail-biting resurfaced. I continued to plan for this much-wanted baby. I had white nursery furniture picked out, and I envisioned a pink and white daisy theme for a girl and a White Sox or baseball theme for a boy. I had everything checked off on the baby store list that I wanted to put on the registry; I was waiting to hear from the adoption agency to use that pricing gun. I had the number of the woman in charge of our infant CPR class where we had gotten certified. She told us we could get donated breast milk at our local hospital for free once we adopted if we wanted. I looked at baby clothes every time I went shopping or went to a craft show. I had resisted the temptation every single time, even though everything was *so* stinkin' cute! Vin was right; we didn't want to jinx anything. I also read about how to introduce the dogs to the new baby. We were all set! All we needed was the baby.

Month after month, we got the phone call from Debbie at the adoption agency telling us we had not been chosen and to keep thinking positively. "We don't know what triggers our birth moms to pick a family." We waited patiently, still hopeful that a birthmother would choose us. Two years seemed to fly by, and to our dismay, no birth mother chose us to be adoptive parents of her child. We received our final phone call from Debbie. Our contract was up, and we could extend it for another six months for a fee, but there were no guarantees. Once again, emotionally and financially tapped out.

I had had enough. I felt like such a loser. No one thought we were suitable enough to parent their child. I had made all these plans for nothing. Maybe the adoption agency could smell our desperation and took advantage of us. I felt so positive that this was God's plan for us. We briefly discussed foster care again with our social worker but collectively decided this was not a good fit for us as the goal of foster care was to return the child to their birth parent. In my heart, I knew I could not do that; I would not want to give the child up, so we opted out of foster care. How dare I get my hopes up? All the planning I had done, the picking of names, the bedding, the clothes, the toys, for what?

CHAPTER 13

What I did know was that we now had to face the rest of our lives alone. We would never have the joy of having a biological child or loving an adopted child as our own. I was mad at myself for getting my hopes up. I was so sure a birthmother would pick us. I felt like a fool. A sucker. A complete loser. Depression and anxiety started creeping in again. I needed to talk to Katherine and Dr. Emmerson. I wondered how Vinny was feeling; he never talked about how he was feeling.

At an all-time low, I was once again defeated, licking my wounds when an email popped up in my inbox. The email read, *"In honor of all that made your family possible, please make a gift in support to Warm Hugs Adoption Agency."* I just about flew through the roof. I was furious! *Are you freaking kidding me?* I fired off an email to Debbie at Warm Hugs Adoption Agency:

> *Dear Debbie,*
>
> *I know this is not your fault, but I just had to bring this to your attention and have you reiterate my displeasure to the person responsible for sending this email. We were **not** fortunate enough to adopt through Warm Hugs Adoption Agency and wish to be removed from all further emails from your agency. Our wounds are still fresh, having learned less than two weeks ago that we were not chosen as adoptive parents and would not be adopting a baby. I ask that you take this matter up with the person responsible for soliciting further donations and express the hurt she has erroneously inflicted on myself and my husband.*
>
> *We respectfully ask that Warm Hugs Adoption Agency be more diligent in keeping their lists up to date as not to inflict this undue pain on anyone else who was not chosen to be adoptive parents.*
>
> *Sincerely,*
> *Jessica Fontana*

With tears streaming down my face, I hit send, closed my laptop, and retreated to my bedroom. I laid on my bed with my pups and cried for hours. I contemplated why I thought this time would be different. Why was I so hopeful this time? I felt like an idiot. I did not understand why God did not want us to have children. When I get to Heaven, that's the first question I'm going to ask God. Why couldn't I be a mom? That is if I make it there.

CHAPTER 13

Carrot Cake

Ingredients:

3 cups flour
3 teaspoons baking powder
2 teaspoons baking soda
1 teaspoon salt
2 teaspoons cinnamon
2 cups sugar
1 1/2 cups vegetable oil
3 cups grated raw carrots
4 eggs beaten
3/4 chopped walnuts
3/4 cup golden raisins

Directions:

Sift flour once and add baking powder, baking soda, salt, and cinnamon.

Combine sugar and oil, mix well by hand, add eggs one at a time and beat with a mixer after each egg.

Add carrots to the sugar and oil mixture, stir by hand. Add dry ingredients slowly and blend by hand. Add in walnuts and raisins, stir.

Pour into greased Bundt pan. Bake at 350 degrees for 40-50 minutes. Check after 30 minutes, may need more or less time. The cake is done when a toothpick inserted comes out clean.

Cream Cheese Frosting:

Ingredients:

8 ounces cream cheese, softened
1/4 cup butter, softened
2 tablespoons sour cream
1 tablespoon vanilla extract
4 cups powdered sugar

<u>Directions:</u>

Add the cream cheese, butter, sour cream, and vanilla to a stand mixer and beat until light and fluffy. Add in the powdered sugar one cup at a time until smooth and incorporated.

Spread on cooled cake. Top with additional walnuts if desired.

Enjoy! Jessica

Chapter 14

Shortly after our devastating disappointment of not becoming adoptive parents, Vin's father became very ill, suffered a massive stroke, and passed away. Vin stayed at his mom's house, helping her with arrangements. I made the trip out for the funeral. The church was packed, a testament to the man he was, the lives he touched, and how many people would miss him. Although our family would sorely miss him, we had the peace knowing he would have eternal life with God

After the funeral, I had to make the trek home. Vin stayed to help his mom for another week, along with his siblings. Upon arriving home, my pups greeted me with wagging tails, barks, and Pippy's bark/howl- he missed his mommy. I was emotionally exhausted from the day's events, and within a few minutes of being with my pups, I could already feel the stress of the day leaving my body. I fed them, and we sat down and snuggled on the couch. My phone rang, and I could see it was my friend Katherine calling.

"Hi, Katherine," I said as I answered the phone.

"Hi, Jessica, how are you?"

"Unfortunately, I just arrived home from my father-in-law's funeral." I went on to tell her about the stroke and that he had passed peacefully. "Also, our adoption contract ended, and we were not chosen. It's been a pretty stressful and emotional time. How is your mom doing?" Katherine had been back in her hometown, helping her father take care of her mother, who had cancer.

"My mom is doing better, thanks for asking. I'm sorry the adoption didn't work out for you. I know you and Vinny would have been great parents."

"Thanks, Katherine; I think so too. I'm still processing it. I was so hopeful we would be chosen. I just don't understand why we are not able to be parents. Enough about me; I haven't talked to you in forever. What's happening in your life?"

"Well," she sighed and hesitated. "I came home a few days ago because I was not feeling well. I've lost a lot of weight, lack an appetite, and I have back pain. I thought it was the stress of taking care of my mom. I went to the doctor and had some testing done. Jessica, I have stage four pancreatic cancer."

I was at a loss for words. I didn't know what to say except, "I'm so sorry, Katherine. Is there anything I can do? What sort of treatment are the doctors going to give you?"

"I'm starting chemo tomorrow, but the prognosis doesn't look good. The doctor could not give me a timeframe. I'm thinking about eighteen months."

I was in shock. "I'm so sorry, Katherine." I didn't know what else to say, afraid to say the wrong thing. What do you tell a person who has just been handed a death sentence? "I'll call you in a few days to check up on you. I love you, Katherine."

"Okay, I love you too, Jess. I'm sorry the adoption didn't work out."

"Thanks. I'll talk to you in a few days. Good luck with your chemo treatments."

That was the last time I spoke to her. Every time I called, I got her voicemail and never received a call back. I thought she wasn't feeling up to talking. I sent her a get-well card that I had made.

It had been a couple of weeks since our phone call; when I was scrolling through social media, I saw a post from a childhood friend of hers asking for prayers for Katherine and her

CHAPTER 14

husband. I knew Elizabeth through Katherine, and I immediately contacted her, not knowing if she would remember me, as we had only met once. To my relief, she got back to me quickly and said Katherine was not doing well and probably would not make it through the night. I was in shock and devastated. I should have been more persistent with my calling or at least made the trip back home to see her. Elizabeth told me that Katherine had made peace with God, and she was ready to go. She passed peacefully that evening with her husband and father at her side. I found out at the funeral that Katherine's mother had passed away a week before she did. At least she would be with her mother, I thought, and that gave me some peace. I still felt horrible and guilty that I had not made an effort to see her, something I would regret for the rest of my life. I had let down my person. I vowed then and there never to let that happen again. I would make an effort to spend time with the people I loved. I was grieving from my father-in-law's recent loss and the failed adoption, and now my best friend.

Having lost both my father-in-law and best friend within two weeks of each other, Vinny and I decided we wanted to move back to be closer to family. Vinny decided to look for a job back where we had lived.

MY SECRET GRIEF

Listy - Angel Wings

Ingredients:

1/2 stick butter
2 1/2 cups four (sifted)
Pinch of salt
1 tablespoon sugar
1 tablespoon rum or brandy
2 egg yolks
3/4 cup half & half
Few drops of vanilla extract

Directions:

Mix the above ingredients and let the dough stand for at least 2 hours or more. Then roll out thin and cut out into squares. Make two slits in each square. Fry in hot grease or lard, turning once. Drain well on paper towels. Sprinkle with powdered sugar.

Enjoy! Jessica

Chapter 15

I saw Dr. Emmerson monthly now, and it was time for another appointment. I arrived at her office building at 9 a.m. I signed in and waited for the nursing assistant to call my name.

"Jessica?" The nursing assistant said. I stood up, smiled, and followed her to the back to get my weight and vitals once again. "Are you having any problems with the medication Dr. Emmerson has you on?"

"No, I'm good." She led me to Dr. Emmerson's office.

"Good morning Jessica. I'm just finishing with an email I needed to address this morning. I'll be right with you, have a seat, and make yourself comfortable."

I watched as her well-manicured fingers flew across the keyboard. I thought Dr. Emmerson was pretty—she was plain but pretty. Today she was wearing black-rimmed glasses, which made her look cute, nerdy, and smart all at the same time. In less than a minute, she was done and put her full attention on me.

"How has your month been, Jessica? Tell me what's going on."

"Well, I said, letting out a big sigh, it's been a rough month. First, our adoption contract ended, and we were not chosen. We are not adopting a child. We decided not to extend the contract because the agency could not guarantee us a placement. I feel like we were swindled."

"I'm sorry, Jessica."

"Second, my father-in-law had a massive stroke and passed away. He was a wonderful man, and I miss him very much. The church where we had the funeral was packed, a testament to the man he was. Vinny is staying with his mom this week, helping her with paperwork and packing up some of his dad's things to donate to charity. Third, the icing on the cake, my best friend Katherine passed away from pancreatic cancer. She thought she had about eighteen months, but she succumbed to cancer within two weeks." My voice was quiet, and I continued speaking, staring at the floor. "I had spoken to her on the phone the evening of my father-in-law's funeral, and she told me the news. She was starting chemo the following day. I spoke with her husband at the funeral, and the cancer was too advanced for the chemo to do any good, and they stopped treatment. She was in hospice for about two weeks and wasn't coherent. I didn't know. I had called, but she never called me back. I guess she couldn't. So, I've been down in the dumps."

"I'm so sorry, Jessica, that's quite a bit to deal with."

"Un-huh." I grabbed the tissue box as tears were flowing now. "My trichotillomania has started back up. It's not as severe as it has been in the past. I've bitten off all my nails to the point where my fingers hurt. I've been journaling my feelings in my book like you taught me, and I have been using the breathing exercises. It seems to help the trichotillomania. I've been trying to stay positive by looking at pictures of my father-in-law and Katherine. I want to remember the time I spent with them and the happy memories we shared."

"That's great, Jessica. I'm glad the de-stressing techniques are helping."

"How is Vinny handling all of this loss?" She asked.

"Vinny was sad, of course, but he is a very optimistic guy and seems to roll with it. He has a strong faith and is at peace, knowing his father is with God. As far as the baby, I'm not sure; he doesn't mention it. I think he doesn't want to upset me."

CHAPTER 15

Dr. Emmerson transitioned to focusing on each one of my stressors for the month.

"It sounds like you are processing your father-in-law's and best friend's deaths by remembering good things about them. Going through pictures is a great way to do that. If you need me or want to talk more about them, you can always make an appointment. No need to wait for your monthly appointment."

"Okay, thank you. I'll keep that in mind."

"Jessica, what would you like your family and friends to know about being childless, not by choice. What would you say to them? When you go home, I want you to write it in your journal. You may share it with your family and friends if and when you are ready or not at all."

"Okay, I will do that. The writing definitely helps."

"Looks like your session is up. I have you on the calendar for next month. Please, if you need to talk in the meantime, don't hesitate to make an appointment."

"Sounds good. Thank you."

When I arrived home, I went straight to my bedroom and retrieved my journal. I sat on the couch and wrote in my journal the rest of the afternoon with Pippy and Tigger by my side.

Journal entry: There is a lot of emotion every day for those of us who are childless, not by choice. Things people say—most of the time, I don't think it's meant to be mean—but sometimes people talk without thinking first. Some comments strike a nerve. These are just some of the feelings and emotions I have experienced or not experienced by not being able to have children. Imagine your life for five minutes, only five if you were childless, not by choice. All the things you may have missed or not experienced because you didn't have children. Think of all the people you know. How many of them do you know because of your children? All the photos and the vacations you didn't take because you didn't have children.

I never had a positive pregnancy test to share with my husband. I never got to share the *good news* with anyone that we were pregnant. I didn't get to feel what it's like to be pregnant, *the good and the bad.* I never got to feel a life growing inside of me. I never got to feel the first movement or kick. There was no morning sickness, no cravings, and no missed menstrual cycles. I did not experience my own baby shower and share this joyful experience with my friends and family members, who mean the most to me. I did not get to experience the pain of birth (maybe this one is ok). Likewise, not experiencing the pain, I also didn't get to experience the joyous payoff of giving birth. I didn't get to hear my baby's first cry. I didn't get to see my baby's face for the first time and instantly fall in love. I didn't get to see my baby's first smile or be proud of them when they reached their milestones like sitting up, rolling over, crawling, walking, getting their first tooth, or the first haircut.

I didn't get to see their personality develop and see what kinds of foods they liked or disliked. I didn't get to see the look on their face when they first recognized me or my husband or other family members. I didn't get to hear them laugh, coo, or cry. I didn't get to watch them sleeping peacefully in their crib. I didn't get to experience getting up in the middle of the night for a feeding or diaper change. I didn't get to kiss their boo-boos, wipe their tears, or comfort them when they were hurting. I didn't get to watch them grow and see the people they became. I didn't get to see what interested them, what friends they had, what career or spouse they chose.

I didn't get to buy them presents for their birthday or Christmas and see the look on their face when they opened them. I didn't get to experience a vacation with them, or any memories for that matter. I didn't get to meet their friends or their friend's parents. I didn't get to go to school plays, sporting events, or any extracurricular activities. I didn't see how they were progressing in school and what their teachers thought of them. I didn't get to see them interact with others.

CHAPTER 15

I didn't get to see them graduate from school. I didn't get to send them to college and then watch them graduate. I didn't get to see them get married and start a life of their own. I didn't get to be a grandma. I didn't get to celebrate Mother's Day. I only have one picture of my child, *one.*

I just want people to be sensitive to those who don't have children, not by choice. I want people to understand it is hard for us to go to your child's birthday party. Of course, we want to be there; you are our friend or family; we love your child; we love you. Keep in mind that it is a constant reminder of what we don't have. *It hurts.* Every milestone your child achieves, our child didn't. We didn't get to experience any of those things even though we wanted to.

For many of us, childless people, it is challenging for us to get ourselves to go to your child's event. But even if we skip a few, please keep asking. We will get better. The pain will never go away, there are constant reminders everywhere every day, but all I ask is to be sensitive to our situation. Let us be a part of your child's life. We are not invisible.

I'm not going to lie; it's a roller coaster ride. There are some days I'm depressed, and I'm down in that hole again, and I can't get out, or I don't want to get out. I want to hide from the pain. Don't let it consume me. Don't let me get buried. I have a lot of love to give but often keep my feelings inside because the hurt is immense. I'm afraid to love fully because I know this child is yours and not mine and will never be mine. I keep my heart guarded, and I keep a distance. I will never have that mother-child bond or relationship. I have to find other ways to fill that hole in my heart. I have to find a reason to get up in the morning. I don't have anyone dependent on me, I don't feel I have anyone that really needs me, and everyone should feel needed, wanted, and loved.

Don't even get me started on the holidays. Mother's Day is a particular sore spot for me. It is a tough day. It is one of the days out of the year that is amplified in my head that I am not a mom. One time at a family gathering, when everyone arrived, we were all greeting each other with our usual hug and kiss and a Happy Mother's Day to those who were moms, and Mindi said to me, "Happy Mothe…, oh wait, you're not a mom". *OUCH!!!!!* It was like she stabbed me right in the heart and nailed me to the wall. It ruined the entire day for me. I just wanted to crawl in a hole somewhere and cry. But instead, I had to play it off, hold back the tears and pretend those words didn't hurt me, but they did. They really, really did. I cried an ocean of tears when I got home.

Let me tell you what Vin and I experienced together and separately—countless negative pregnancy tests. Wishful hoping and thinking that maybe this month would be the month that we were pregnant only to be disappointed when Aunt Flo showed up, again and again, month after month. I endured many medical procedures, everything from acupuncture, medicines, IVF shots, egg harvesting, and implantation, which resulted in no baby. The countless trips to the OBGYN and fertility clinics with pregnant women everywhere! We also experienced failed attempts at adoption. All of this was expensive and financially devastating. We were genuinely happy for each friend and family member that got pregnant and had a baby. The last time I counted, there were at least 50 newborns added to our life during our 20-year infertility struggle. Silently we suffered; when would it be our turn? What will our baby shower be like? I feel so foolish for thinking I would be a mom someday when God had other plans for my life.

Think back on your life. Subtract your children. Subtract all the people in your life you have met because of your children. Subtract all the vacations taken with your children. Subtract all the school events your children were in. Subtract all the photos with your children. Subtract all of the memories with your children, good and bad. Can you even do it? How do you feel? This is what it's like for people who are childless, not by choice. We are on the outside looking in, keeping our grief a secret.

CHAPTER 15

Jelly Roll Cake

Ingredients:

3 large eggs
1 cup granulated sugar
1/4 cup cold water
3/4 cup all-purpose flour
2 teaspoons baking powder
1 pinch salt
1 teaspoon vanilla or almond extract
Powdered sugar
1 cup raspberry preserves, more if needed or desired

Directions:

- Preheat oven to 400 degrees

- Prepare jelly roll pan – lined with parchment paper and generally grease and flour or spray with cooking spray.

- In a medium bowl, beat the eggs with an electric mixer until lemon colored, approximately 3-4 minutes. Slowly add the sugar while mixing. Beat in the water and vanilla. Gradually add the flour, baking powder, and salt. Beat until smooth.

- Pour evenly into the prepared pan. Bake 12-15 minutes.

- Loosen edges of the cake with a knife. Immediately after removing the pan from the oven, place a clean kitchen towel that has been dusted with powdered sugar over the top of the jelly roll pan. Turn the pan upside down on the towel. Carefully remove wax paper. While still hot, roll the cake up tightly on the small end. Let cool thoroughly. Then, unroll the cake and remove the towel.

- In a small bowl, beat raspberry preserves thoroughly and spread over the entire cake. Roll up the cake again from the small end and dust with powdered sugar. Cover and chill several hours or overnight. Before serving, cut a little off the ends to give it a clean look. Dust with more powdered sugar if desired. Slice and enjoy!

Enjoy! Jessica

Chapter 16

Within a few months, and with the help of a recruiter, Vinny found a great job. We were back by family, where we belonged.

Vinny always took a lot of naps since before I even met him. I never really thought much about it; some people just need more sleep. He liked to stay up late and never slept well through the night. I never gave it a second thought.

Vinny had been up most of the night with back pain. He thought he was suffering from a kidney stone, which he had had in the past. In recent months Vinny had not been sleeping, had lost a lot of weight, and was hot all the time, sweating after meals and during his sleep. Despite me telling him to make an appointment, he hadn't. Now the pain was too much for him to handle, and we headed to the urgent care center.

While in the waiting room, my phone rang. It was Vinny's cousin from Wisconsin.

"Hi, Rebecca! I said joyfully. "How are you?"

"Hi, Jessica." I could hear her crying; this was not going to be good news. "I wanted to let you know that my dad passed away, suddenly, of a heart attack this morning."

"I'm so sorry. Are you okay? What do you need me to do for you?"

"Thank you. I'm getting through it the best I can, still a little shocked. Could you tell Vinny and call Aunt Rose and tell her the news and have her call the rest of the family?"

"Of course, no problem, I'm happy to help. I'm at urgent care with Vinny right now. He has a kidney stone. I'll call his mom so she can call the family. I'm so sorry, Rebecca. I loved Uncle Martin. He was a good guy."

"Thanks, Jessica. I'll call you when I have the funeral details. I hope Vinny feels better soon."

"Thanks. Bye."

"Vinny, I'm sorry to say, your Uncle Martin passed away from a heart attack this morning. I have to call your mom and let her know."

"Thanks, Jess. We should go over to her house after I see the doctor. I'll probably have to drive her to Wisconsin."

"We'll see what the doctor says first. We can always ask Gino to drive her."

The nurse had arrived to take down the medical history and Vinny's vitals.

"The doctor will be in shortly to see you." She said.

"Okay, thank you."

There was a knock at the door. "Come in," Vin said.

"Hi, I'm Dr. McCormick. I'll be taking care of you today. You think you have a kidney stone?"

"Yes, I get them all the time. This one, though, I just can't seem to pass. I've had pain in my back and left side for months."

She started poking around, and Vinny was in an extreme amount of pain. "I'm going to order some bloodwork and take a look. I will send the nurse in to draw the blood, and I'll be back after I take a look at it."

"Sounds good."

While Vinny was speaking to the nurse and getting his blood drawn, I called my mother-in-law to tell her the sad news of Uncle Martin's passing. When I turned back to Vinny, the nurse left with several vials of Vinny's blood.

CHAPTER 16

The nurse came back in and said, "We are taking you for a CT Scan in a little bit to take a look around your kidneys and abdomen."

"How long do you think it's going to take?" I asked.

"The test will take about half an hour, but we are a little backed up, so about an hour or so."

"Okay, thanks. Vin, I'm going to run to the store down the street and see if I can find a black top to wear to the funeral. I don't have one in my closet that will fit me. Text me after your scan if I'm not back."

"Okay."

I left the urgent care and went to the plus-size store down the street. I was only in the store for about fifteen minutes and had found what I was looking for, a simple black blouse. I decided to drive back to the house and check on Pippy and Tigger as Tigger had not been acting his usual self lately. I decided to eat something for lunch while I was there. I was spending time with the pups when I got a text from Vin. *Are you done shopping? Come back to urgent care.* I texted back, *on my way.*

I arrived at the urgent care and walked up to the reception desk. "I left to run an errand while my husband was getting a CT scan. Can someone take me back to his room?"

"Sure, what is the last name?"

"Fontana."

"Vincenzo?"

"Yes."

The receptionist called back to the treatment area, and within a minute, the nurse was there to take me back to Vinny. When I entered the room, Vin was lying in bed, very pale. He looked like he had been crying.

"What's wrong, Vin? Are you okay? Are you in pain?" He couldn't speak. He opened his mouth, but no words were coming out. He reached for my hand. As I stood there holding his hand, I knew something was terribly wrong. Dr. McCormick appeared.

"Hi, Jessica. Vinny does not have a kidney stone. He has a very high white blood count; we think he has lymphoma. We are transporting him to the Emergency Room by ambulance. You can meet him there."

I was in shock but shook my head in agreement. I kissed Vinny on the forehead as the paramedics arrived with the gurney to take him to the Emergency Room. Once safely in the ambulance, I briskly walked to my car and drove to the hospital. The parking lot was packed, and I had to park far away. I still made it to the Emergency Room before Vinny.

I sat in the ER waiting room, anticipating Vin's arrival, still in shock.

"May I get you anything, dear?" An elderly voice interrupted my thoughts.

"No, thank you. I'm waiting for my husband to arrive by ambulance."

"My name is Anne, and I'm one of the volunteers here at the hospital. What is your husband's name?"

"Vincenzo Fontana."

"When your husband arrives, I will bring you to his room. If you need anything, I'll be right over there; just ask."

"Okay, thank you," I said softly, trying my best not to cry. I'm sure the worry in my voice was prominent.

About ten minutes later, Anne came and retrieved me and walked me to Vinny. It seemed like we were walking forever through a long maze of hallways until we finally reached his room. "Here he is, dear."

"Thank you," I replied. Vinny and I sat in silence for a long time. He was so pale and thin, and he looked so tired and worried. It reminded me of when my dad was sick and in the hospital. I think we were both still in shock. Tears rolled down my face as I sat across from him. Nurses were in and out, hooking up wires and machines to monitor him. I

CHAPTER 16

stayed out of the way. They asked a million questions, and we signed lots of papers. Everything seemed to be going in slow motion, and at the same time, I don't think I comprehended much of what they were saying. I was shivering and rubbing my upper arms.

Vinnie's family was on their way out of town to help Aunt Lillian with the funeral preparations. More nurses and hospital staff entered and left his room, and we signed more paperwork as we waited for the porter to take him for a CT scan.

I was still cold and had to find a bathroom. "I'll be right back, honey."

"Okay. I'll be right here," he said playfully. He was always using his sense of humor to deflect what he was really feeling. I searched for a bathroom and found one down the hall and quickly ducked in to use it, trying to be as fast as I could so I could get back to Vinny. Such a relief! Now, if I could just get warm.

Shortly after returning to Vinny's room, the porter came and wheeled him away for the CAT scan. "We'll have him back in thirty to forty-five minutes," the nurse told me.

"No problem," I said. Vin waved goodbye as they wheeled him out of the room. Tears rolled down my face, and I couldn't stop them. I got up and grabbed some tissue. Then I noticed an older man who had been walking up and down the hallway, passing by Vinny's room several times. He was wearing a plaid shirt, blue jeans, and a baseball cap. He looked a lot like my father-in-law, dressed like him, and walked like him. It was uncanny. That was the moment I knew I was not alone. Even though Vinny's father had passed away a couple of years earlier, I knew that he was there for Vinny, and I felt a little bit of peace. I was still cold but a little calmer knowing his dad was there in spirit.

An hour and a half later, I was getting concerned; *where was Vinny?* The nurse came in and informed me there was a backup in the CAT Scan Department and that he should be back soon. "Is there anything I can get for you?" she asked.

I replied, "Do you happen to have a blanket? It's freezing in here."

"Sure, let me go get a warm one for you." She was back five minutes later with a toasty warm blanket. I could feel the warmth as I wrapped it around myself, yet I continued to shiver. Still no Vinny, though. I started to really worry as three hours had passed. While waiting, I must have heard *Braham's Lullaby* play six times. The hospital played this every time a baby was born. Here I wondered if my husband would live or die, and someone else was celebrating the birth of their child. Another daily reminder that I was childless, not by choice. This thought was broken when I heard laughter in the hallway. He must be near, cracking jokes as he often did to mask what he was feeling, which was probably fear. He always tried to make light of bad situations. I was still crying, and my eyes were red. They wheeled him in, got him situated, and hooked the monitors back up to him. We waited for the doctor.

"I told you to go to the doctor months ago; I sensed something was wrong. You thought it would just go away—the lost appetite, the night sweats, the weight loss, the paleness, and the bruising. In the back of my mind, I knew it was something serious. I should have insisted you go to the doctor."

Just then, the doctor came in. It was Julia!

"Hi, guys."

"Hi, Julia!" I got up and hugged her. Some relief came over my body. "I thought you were in New York?"

"I was but ultimately decided I wanted to be back here where I grew up and to be near my family. I'm sorry we lost touch."

"It's okay. We moved around a lot for Vinny's job and didn't let you know."

There was an awkward pause, then she spoke.

CHAPTER 16

"Well, there is no beating around the bush; you have leukemia." BAM!

"Jinxer," Vin replied jokingly, looking my way.

"All the signs were there," I said. "I should have insisted you go to the doctor, but I just didn't want to believe what I was thinking was true. I should have made the appointment myself and not waited until your spleen almost exploded." I was so mad at myself for not making him go to the doctor, angry at him for not going to the doctor, and mad at God. I mean, how much more can I take? I have had my share of loss. My grandmother, then my dad, my baby girl, my father-in-law, my best friend, and now possibly my husband?! Seriously?? He's all I have. He is my entire world; he is absolutely everything to me. Please, please, please don't take him from me. I pleaded all this in my mind to God.

Doctor Julia said, "The good news is that if you're going to have cancer, this is the one to have. There is no cure, but we can keep it in check with a chemo pill. Unfortunately, you will need to take this pill for the rest of your life." In my mind, I was thinking, and just how long is that? But I dared not say it; I didn't want to upset Vinny. "There is no intravenous chemo or radiation or anything like that." Julia explained, more medical mumbo jumbo and that she would be starting Vinny on the chemo pill immediately. He would have a bone marrow biopsy the next morning and be in the hospital for three to four days.

During this time, I had been texting with Gino, who was with the rest of the family at Aunt Lillian's house in Wisconsin, helping with funeral arrangements. I was getting text messages from his sister and mother asking about Vinny's condition. I had to lie and keep saying we didn't know anything yet, even though we had the diagnosis. I didn't want them to worry. They needed to focus on their grief and Aunt Lillian.

The staff transferred Vinny to a regular room. When he was settled, I said goodnight and kissed him goodbye as it was now 9:00 PM. Visiting hours were over, and I had to go home and take care of the dogs. I had called my mom earlier to go over to the house to feed the dogs and let them out. I didn't want to leave them home alone overnight. Vinny was having a bone marrow biopsy in the morning; I didn't want to be there for that. I had heard it was a painful procedure. My friend Katherine had had one when she was diagnosed with breast cancer. Vinny did not do well with pain or needles. I think if he saw how long the needle was for the biopsy, he would pass out, which I guess could be a good thing.

I managed to find my way out of the hospital maze and to my car. By this time, my head was pounding, and I had the worst headache. It felt like my head was going to explode. I hadn't had anything to eat or drink since lunch. With all the stress, I wasn't even thinking about eating. When I got home, the dogs were jumping on me, happy I was back. I read the note my mom had left: The dogs are fed, they both did their business, and I played with them a bit before leaving. They were no trouble. Call me if you need me tomorrow and update me on Vinny. Love, Mom.

My head was still pounding. I drank some water and sat on the couch with my boys. They gave me lots of kisses and then snuggled in my lap and fell asleep. I texted Gino as I didn't think I would be able to talk on the phone without crying. I wrote, *Vinny has cancer, leukemia, but a treatable form. He will be on a chemo pill for the rest of his life. There is no cure. He probably had it since childhood. Can you please wait to tell the family until after the funeral? I don't want the attention taken away from Uncle Martin and his family.*

He texted back. *I'm sorry, Jess, I'll tell them in a couple of days after the funeral. Give my best to Vin. Tell him that I'm praying for him and you.*

Thanks. Goodnight Gino.

Goodnight Jess.

CHAPTER 16

I quickly called my mom and told her the news. With that, I turned off the phone and took the boys up to bed with me. I didn't want to be in that big king-size bed all by myself. I put a glass of water next to my bed, along with a bottle of ibuprofen. I laid there going through the events of the day, feeling the warmth of my dogs, and finally feeling warm myself. My mind was racing. All the "what if" scenarios running through my head. What if Vinny dies? I'm totally screwed. I don't make enough money to support myself. If he can't work, I cannot support both of us on my salary.

I can't even pay the mortgage on my salary. All the things that Vinny does around the house I'm going to have to do. I don't know how to do anything except cooking, clean, and my job. I never finished college. I don't have a college degree; I only have a certificate. What kind of a job am I going to get that can support both of us? I was in full panic mode, worrying that if something happened to Vinny, I would be devastated. I would probably end up homeless. I don't have any children to help take care of me. Between infertility treatments, the 2008 recession, and the failed adoption, we didn't have any savings left. I don't have anyone I can depend on. I don't want to be a burden to anyone physically or financially. I needed to figure out something quickly. I prayed. God, please don't take Vinny away from me. He is my entire world. I would be so lost without him. I need him. I love him. God, please heal him.

I hardly slept. I tossed and turned all night. When morning came, I was surprised I felt better. I wasn't tired, probably running on pure adrenaline. I fed and took care of the dogs. I ate breakfast, which made my headache a little bit better. I called my work and Vinny's work to tell them what was going on and then headed to the hospital.

I was happy I missed the bone marrow biopsy, which I did on purpose. I had heard it was an excruciating procedure, and Vinny told me I was right. I sat next to him the entire day, and we didn't talk much. He slept a little between getting poked and prodded and tried to eat, but he had little appetite. He sat in his bed and watched Jerry Springer on TV. The aroma of disinfectant lingered in my nostrils. By the end of the day, Dr. Julia came for a visit. She informed us that the cancer pill was already working. His spleen was down in size, but it still needed to be monitored. Vinny's color was better too. I spent much of the day on the phone with his HR department, ensuring we filled out all the paperwork. I had about a million questions for them, and they could not have been more helpful or more accommodating. My employer, however, was a different story. They let me take the time I needed, but I did not get paid for the time off. They did not give us vacation time or any paid time off, for that matter—just another circumstance adding to our growing mound of debt.

It was day four, and Vinny was getting ready to be discharged. Dr. Julia was off, and another doctor came in to talk about the chemo pill. It was a specialty drug that would need to be ordered, and it was $12,000 a month! Who can afford that? How much would insurance pay? I had a million questions flying through my brain along with panic that we would be eating cat food and living in a cardboard box in the park. This was going to be financially devastating to us again. I was crying and made many more phone calls to Vinny's HR Department until I resolved all the issues. Vinny was finally discharged. On the way home, I thought about our new normal and just how precious life is.

CHAPTER 16

Jessica's Hot Cocoa Mix

Ingredients:

2 1/2 cups powdered sugar
2 1/2 cups powdered milk
1 cup cocoa (regular or dark)
1 teaspoon salt
2 teaspoons corn starch

Directions:

Add all ingredients to a large mixing bowl and combine with a whisk or add to a blender to combine.
Store in airtight containing in the pantry – keeps for a long time.
When ready to use, add 2-3 tablespoons of hot cocoa mix to 8 ounces of hot water or warm milk. Add more mixture to taste. Stir well to combine. Top with whipped cream or marshmallows. Add crushed peppermint, mini chocolate chips, or colorful jimmies/sprinkles for a festive look.

Enjoy! Jessica

Chapter 17

As time went on, I had to figure out what I would do to make money because my job was not cutting it. I thought about all the things that I enjoy doing, and it all came back to baking. *I enjoyed baking.* I decided that I was going to open up a bakeshop, finally. Even though I had taken the cake decorating courses and knew how to make cakes, I didn't enjoy all the detailed work it took to make the cake beautiful, only for it to be cut and eaten in five minutes. Even though I knew they were beautiful pieces of art, they were meant to be consumed. I decided to go back to something I truly enjoyed and thought about my gram.

Some of my favorite memories were being in the kitchen with her baking cookies. I decided my bakery would sell cookies and small pastries. I knew people liked my baking; I just needed to find the money to open up a tiny shop. That's all I wanted, a little café. I thought a lot about my gram and decided to name my bakery, The Rolling Pin Cookie Cafe. I remember using the rolling pin that my grandfather carved for my grandmother. I still have it, and I still use it to this day. At The Rolling Pin Cookie Café, the menu would include cookies and other small pastries such as cupcakes, gourmet rice crispy treats, as well as good old-fashioned Czech desserts, served with milk, coffee, tea, and hot cocoa in the winter. We would also sell dog treats. We can't forget our dogs; they like goodies too! It would be a little gathering place for family and friends to meet and chat and enjoy a little something sweet.

CHAPTER 17

I envisioned The Rolling Pin Cookie Cafe to be something special. Children would remember this place when they became adults and would bring their children there. I wanted them to remember everything—the smell of cookies baking, the homey décor, the friendly faces. It had to be a place of nostalgia for them—colorful, bright, and full of happy memories. I wanted it to feel like home like they were sitting in their grandma's kitchen—Black and white checkered flooring, white open shelving. Armoires loaded with dry cookie mixes—my recipes— and packaged baked cookies by the dozen or half dozen. Large cookie jars on the counters, and you could pick and choose your dozen—a self-serve edible cookie dough bar with sprinkles and other candy toppings. The decor would be butter yellow, soft pink, and Tiffany blue, soothing and cheery at the same time. I finally had a new dream. What would it take to make this dream happen?

Peanut Butter Dog Treats

Ingredients:

2/3 cup pumpkin puree
1/4 cup peanut butter
2 large eggs
3 cups whole wheat flour, more, as needed

Directions:

1. Preheat oven to 350 degrees F. Line a baking sheet with parchment paper, set aside.

2. In the bowl of an electric mixer fitted with the paddle attachment, beat pumpkin puree, peanut butter, and eggs on medium-high until well combined. Gradually add 2 1/2 cups whole wheat flour at low speed, beating until incorporated. Add an additional 1/4 cup flour at a time just until the dough is no longer sticky.

3. Working on a lightly floured surface, knead the dough 3-4 times until it comes together. Using a rolling pin, roll the dough to 1/4-inch thickness. Using a medium-sized bone-shaped cookie cutter, cut out shapes and place them onto the prepared baking sheet.

4. Place into oven and bake until the edges are golden brown, about 20-25 minutes.

5. Let cool completely.

Pups Enjoy! Jessica

Chapter 18

Vin and I were still adjusting to life after his cancer diagnosis. Life would never be the same. There was no cure for his leukemia, but he could live with it, and he would be on a chemo pill for the rest of his life. However long that was. Vin was able to work remotely from home, which was good because he had every single side effect from his medication. I felt helpless as I watched him suffer daily with nausea, headaches, skin rashes, and excruciating bone, muscle, and joint pain. He was still tired all the time. I could tell he was stressed by the way he was eating. He ate junk food constantly and gained about fifty pounds. At his visits with Dr. Julia, she didn't seem to mind that he was gaining weight. She told us she would rather see him gain weight than lose weight. We celebrated the small wins, he was responding well to treatment, and some of his side effects were going away. We cherished every moment together.

Tigger was acting differently. He was always a happy pup, very chill, but he did not like to get smothered in kisses from me like his brother Pippy did. Tigger didn't want me to hold him, but he did like to sit in Vin's lap and cuddle with him. I noticed a change in Tigger's appetite. Our seemingly always hungry dog was no longer eating as much, and he was drinking more water than usual. I made an appointment to see Dr. Peterson, our veterinarian, and he could see Tigger the next day.

We sat in the waiting room amongst all the other canine and feline patients waiting for our name to be called.

"Tigger?" The vet tech said.

Tigger's ears perked up, and we followed her to the room.

"What brings you and Tigger in today, Mrs. Fontana?

"Tigger isn't quite himself, and I listed off his symptoms to her.

"Okay. Dr. Peterson will be in soon to take a look at him." She gave Tigger a little pat on the head and left the room.

A knock on the door, "Come in," I said.

"Hi, Jessica, hi, Tigger!" Tigger walked over to him, wagging his tail. This was the first veterinarian clinic and doctors my dogs liked and never seemed to show signs of stress when visiting. Dr. Peterson looked him over and felt his abdomen.

"I feel something," he said. "I think we should get an ultrasound." Tigger had not eaten that morning, so Dr. Peterson was able to do an ultrasound right away. "I'll call you this afternoon when I have some results."

"Okay, sounds good." I kissed Tigger on the head and hugged him goodbye. I went about my day and waited for the phone call. The vet tech called four hours later and said I could come and pick up Tigger. I drove right over, anxious to see my little pup. I was escorted to one of the exam rooms and waited for Dr. Peterson and Tigger.

I sat and anxiously awaited my reunion with Tigger. Moments later, Dr. Peterson arrived with Tigger.

Dr. Peterson began, "The ultrasound shows a mass on his spleen and something else behind the spleen. I can't see what it is, and I recommend going for a more specialized ultrasound at the Emergency Vet Clinic."

"What do you think it is," I asked.

"Usually, with a mass like this, it could be cancer, he said, concerned. We need to find out what that other shadow is. Is it a mass or an organ? We can remove the spleen, and Tigger

CHAPTER 18

can live a normal life, but we need to see what is behind the spleen."

"Okay, I will make an appointment with the Emergency Vet Clinic right away. Thank you, Dr. Peterson."

"You're welcome, Jessica." He gave Tigger a little rub on the head, and we left.

I drove home with Tigger in the passenger seat on his favorite pillow. He was always so good in the car and enjoyed looking out the window. When I got home, I called the number of the Emergency Vet Clinic. Dr. Peterson gave me and made an appointment. They couldn't get him in for three weeks. Tigger didn't seem to be in any discomfort, so I agreed.

Three weeks later, Vin, Tigger, and I made the forty-five-minute drive to the Emergency Vet Clinic with the specialized ultrasound machine. We met with the doctor, and he explained what he would be doing. Tigger would get the ultrasound later that day, and we had to leave him there. If all were good, they would take out the spleen that day, and he would recover at the hospital until he was well enough to go home. All of this came with a $3000 price tag, *ouch*. But our little boy was worth every penny. We kissed Tigger goodbye and told him we would see him soon. I will never forget the look on his face as they took him away. He looked as if we were abandoning him. It broke my heart, he had the sweetest little face, and he looked so sad.

Vin and I drove home and agreed that we would pay the money for the surgery because Tigger was only eleven, and the typical lifespan for an Italian Greyhound was fifteen years. He still had a few more years to live. We decided we would not put him down.

We were home, not quite two hours, when my phone rang. I raced to the kitchen island, where I had left my phone. It was Dr. Williams calling. "Jessica? This is Dr. Williams. We have the result of Tigger's ultrasound. I'm sorry to say that it's not good news. Tigger has a second mass attached to the spleen and also attached to other organs. I'm afraid it is inoperable. If we were to do the surgery, Tigger would bleed out and die on the table." Tears were streaming down my face as Vin looked at me, knowing that it was not good news. "Why don't you come back and pick up Tigger, and we can discuss the next steps."

"Okay," I managed to say through my tears. I hung up the phone and grabbed the sides of the island to keep myself from collapsing, hung my head, and cried uncontrollably. Vin walked over and rubbed my back. A couple of minutes later, I gained my composure. Vin and I got into the car and raced back to the clinic to be with our little boy. We arrived at the clinic and anxiously awaited our reunion with Tigger. About ten minutes later, here came Tigger, trying to get to us, pulling the vet tech along with him the best he could for such a little guy. He was so happy to see us, and we were delighted to see him. He jumped into Vin's arms and proceeded to lick Vin's face all over, which was unusual for Tigger. I'm sure Tigger had been scared of being there, poked and prodded, they shaved his belly, and who knows what else. The vet tech took us back to Dr. William's office. He pulled up the ultrasound and showed us the masses behind the spleen. Dr. Williams said, "My recommendation is to take him home, love him, spoil him, and give him anything he will eat, even if it's a hamburger from a fast-food restaurant."

"How long does he have?" I asked.

"It's hard to tell; it could be a couple of days, a couple of weeks, or a couple of months." We took Tigger home to love and spoil him.

Our precious Tigger lasted another five months, and we even celebrated his 12th birthday. He had his ups and downs, but he rarely complained. He went in monthly to see Dr. Peterson to get his nails clipped and always seemed happy to see him and his staff, even though each time he was skinnier than the last. He was still eating, at least a little bit, and he

CHAPTER 18

was engaging with us. Finally came the day we were dreading. Tigger seemed to be in a lot of discomfort, his abdomen was distended, and he acted aggressively towards Pippy. He could no longer go up the stairs or lift his leg to pee and stayed in his crate most of the day sleeping. His appetite was non-existent. I was relieved that Vin and I worked at home so we could tend to Tigger's every need. I called Dr. Peterson and scheduled Tigger to be put down the following Monday if he made it through the weekend. We would be able to spend the entire weekend with him, showing him how much we loved him and making him as comfortable as possible. I took tons of pictures of him and kissed him a lot even though he didn't like it. I told him I loved him very much, and I thanked him for letting me be his mom. I just didn't want him to suffer anymore.

Monday came, and the day flew by, and the time I was dreading all day was here. It was time to see Dr. Peterson and the staff. We went as a family, Vin, myself, Tigger, and Pippy, and brought Tigger's bed and favorite blankie. The receptionist escorted us to the room with the oversized comfy couch. Tigger seemed so happy that it broke my heart. His tail was wagging, and he seemed to have some pep in his step. He had acted like he was in discomfort all weekend, had not eaten, and had very little water to drink. Pippy was uncharacteristically calm; Dr. Peterson and his staff had a way with the animals. They took Tigger away to put in the IV, and he was gone a while as they had a hard time finding a vein, most likely due to dehydration. Finally, they brought him back and placed him in his bed. I covered him up with his blankie.

I could not stop crying, wondering if I was doing the right thing. His abdomen was huge, and he had difficulty walking. I kept with my decision that he was suffering and in pain, although he barely let on. I asked Dr. Peterson one last time.

"Dr. Peterson, I don't know if I'm doing the right thing. He seems so happy today."

"Animals showing pain is a sign of weakness and makes them an easy target for prey in the wild. It's instinctual for him to act stoic." I remember how much pain Vin had when his spleen was enlarged and thought Tigger was no different.

"He's not going to get better, right, Dr. Peterson?"

"No, Jessica, he is not going to get better. If his spleen ruptures, he will bleed internally, collapse and die."

"Okay. I don't want him to go through that. I think it's best to continue with the procedure while he seems to be happy."

Vinny sat crying next to Tigger and stroked his back. Pippy sat next to Tigger quietly. I sat in front of him. I stroked his head, kissed him a million times, and told him that I loved him a million times. I told him he was a good boy and to go to sleep. He looked at me the entire time as Dr. Peterson slowly injected the medicine that would stop his heart. A few moments later, I saw his eyes dilate, his body went limp, and he was gone. Dr. Peterson listened to his heart and said, "Tigger has passed. I'm very sorry, he was a good, sweet boy, and you gave him a good life. I'm very sorry for your loss," and he left the room. The vet tech told us to take as much time as we needed. I sat and held Tigger for a while. Vinny sat next to me with his arm around me, rubbing my shoulder. We were both crying. I kissed him one last time, said to him, "I love you, Tigger; go look for Papa and Katherine." Followed by, "I'll see you when I see you, my precious sweet boy," and handed him to the vet tech. I picked up Pippy, and we left as a smaller family. The ride home was quiet, and I hugged and held Pippy all the way home.

As I sat in my recliner crying and holding Pippy, the clouds rolled in, and it began to rain. There had been no rain in the forecast that day. I watched as it poured for about fifteen minutes, and then it stopped, typical for Chicago weather. The clouds parted, and the sun started to peek out. I got up and stood by the patio door and saw the biggest rainbow against the still-grey sky. I grabbed my camera and took a picture.

CHAPTER 18

Tigger was telling me he made it over the rainbow bridge. He was no longer suffering, and I knew he was with my friend Katherine and Papa, and he was going to be okay. "I'll see you when I see you, sweet Tigger boy. I love you."

Less than two weeks after putting Tigger down, we were all still grieving, even Pippy. He kept looking for Tigger upstairs and in his crate, and his appetite was low. At first, I thought he was grieving, like Vin and myself, over the loss of his friend. He is an Italian Greyhound, and he had always been thin—all skin and muscle—but now he was thinner than usual. I had also noticed that he was vomiting up yellow bile in the morning. I decided to make an appointment with Dr. Peterson to check him out.

The next day Dr. Peterson did bloodwork, which came back normal for an almost fifteen-year-old dog. We both chalked it up to Pippy missing Tigger. Dr. Peterson said to keep an eye on him and to call if anything else came up. I agreed.

Over the next couple of weeks, Pippy's appetite decreased even further. I thought that since we had been spoiling both dogs in Tigger's final days, giving them anything, they would eat, that he just was being stubborn and didn't want to eat his dog food anymore. I made him chicken and gave him vegetables and pumpkin, all his favorites, and he ate this for a couple of weeks. When that stopped working, I changed his food to a fresh pet food I could buy at my local pet store. This was favorable for another couple of weeks, and then he started being picky about his food again and was still vomiting the bile in the morning. Now he started having diarrhea and absolutely refused to eat his pumpkin puree, which he loved and had always fixed his bowel issues. As I would do anything for my furry four-legged kids, I researched and bought all kinds of "fixes" at the pet store for diarrhea, with only minimal results—time to go back and see Dr. Peterson.

Dr. Peterson ran more tests and took a biopsy of a lump Pippy had had on his abdomen for a long time. "The biopsy came back inconclusive. However, with his symptoms, he may have stomach cancer," Dr. Peterson said. With Pippy's advanced age of 15, we decided to do nothing, not put him through any sort of surgery. There was no evidence that any kind of operation would prolong his life. He was still eating a little, playing, and engaging with us. Dr. Peterson said to take our senior dog home, continue to love and spoil him and bring him in if his appetite or diarrhea worsened. He sent us home with some medication.

We enjoyed Pippy for seven more months. His appetite decreased even further, but he was still happy and engaging with us until April, Good Friday, to be exact. Pippy became very lethargic. His head was scorching hot, and he slept in his bed the entire day. I had kissed him a lot that day, petted him, and tried to comfort him. I made the dreaded call to Dr. Peterson, and I told him that I think this is it. Pippy has not eaten in 48 hours and has had nothing to drink for 24 hours. He was sleeping all day, his head was very hot, and I didn't know if he would make it through the night. It was Easter weekend, and I had made an appointment for him to be put down on the following Monday if he made it through the weekend. I felt he was suffering and could not bear for him to have another day like today. I emailed my boss and let her know what was happening and that I would be taking Monday off of work to spend the last day with my dog.

Good Friday evening, around 7 p.m., Pippy was up, walking around, drinking a lot, and even eating a little bit. He was engaging with us and was very, very loving, and he snuggled on my lap for the rest of the night. I called my mom and the rest of the family and told them Pippy was very sick. I would not be hosting Easter, but we could all meet at a restaurant for Easter Brunch. If anyone wanted to come back to the house to say goodbye to Pippy, they were welcome to do so.

That evening I slept downstairs on the couch; Pippy lay asleep on my recliner. He made it through the night. Saturday

CHAPTER 18

morning Pippy did not want to get out of bed. I let him lay on my recliner all day. I made him comfortable and brought him his favorite teddy bear. Pippy again slept most of the day, and I kissed him many times throughout the day and told him that I loved him. He did not eat and drank minimal that day. On Easter Sunday, it was much of the same. We met our family for Easter Brunch but did not stay long, as I wanted to get back to Pippy. Everyone came back to our house, and we sat and talked. Pippy had some pep in his step and was feeling better. He still didn't eat, but he drank a little. He was engaging with everyone, and his tail was wagging. Everyone had a chance to say goodbye to him that day.

Monday arrived too quickly. I held him as much as he would let me. I kissed him and told him how much I loved him and that he was a good boy. He didn't want to eat or drink, and he slept most of the day, and I took lots and lots of pictures. Late afternoon was upon us, time to take Pippy to see Dr. Peterson one last time. We again were in the room with the comfy couch. We brought his bed, blanket, and favorite teddy bear. The vet tech took him in the back to put in his IV. When she brought Pippy back, I wrapped him in his blanket and held him on my lap. I told him over and over again how much I loved him and kissed the top of his head. I told him how much joy he brought to my life for the last fifteen years and seven months.

Vinny sat in front of Pippy, petted his head, rubbed his velvet ears, kissed his snout, and rubbed him under the chin, which Pippy had always enjoyed. Dr. Peterson administered the medication. I whispered into his ear; I love you, sweet boy. Find Tigger, Papa, and Katherine. I will see you when I see you. I felt his body go limp, and I sobbed and sobbed. Dr. Peterson checked his heart rate and told us he was gone. He again said he was sorry for our loss, and Pippy had a good long life, and he knew how much we loved him. With that, Dr. Peterson left the room, and we said our final goodbyes to

Pippy. I kissed and hugged him one last time, as did Vinny, and then I handed him over to the vet tech. Vin and I left and cried all the way home.

It was weird walking into the house. It was quiet, and no jumping dog was wagging his tail there to greet us. The house was silent. I sat in my recliner, holding Pippy's teddy bear, and cried.

The next two weeks were an adjustment. We had known the end was coming. We were a little more prepared this time, but a loss is a loss. We were still grieving, and we knew we didn't want another dog, at least for a while. I started packing up Tigger's and Pippy's toys, clothes, and other accessories, deciding what I would keep and what I would donate to the rescue group where we had rescued them. I decided to keep the bed they both shared and took it out onto the patio to shake it out. I started shaking it, and a tiny bone-shaped treat flew out. I laughed out loud. Pippy was always "hiding" his dog treats around the house, in cabinet corners, corners of the stairs, in the couch, and in his bed. Tigger usually found them and ate them. I guess Pippy hid this one after Tigger's passing. I looked up, and at that exact moment, a red cardinal flew by and sat in a nearby tree. I finally had my sign that Pippy was okay. I said out loud, "Hi, Pippy," and then the cardinal flew away.

From that day forward, every single day, I see a male and female cardinal in my yard. I say hello to them and call them Pippy and Tigger. Even though my dogs were both males, I like to think the female cardinal is Tigger, as they are almost the same color. I believe this is Pippy and Tigger's way of telling me *we are okay, mom, we are still here watching over you, and we love you.*

CHAPTER 18

Lip Smackin' Chicken Dog Biscuits

Ingredients:

1 1/4 cups whole wheat flour
3 tablespoons oil
1/3 cup chicken broth or stock

Directions:

Preheat oven to 350 degrees. Line baking sheet with parchment paper.

Mix all ingredients in a bowl.

Roll out on a lightly floured surface to 1/8 inch thick.

Using a medium-sized bone-shaped cookie cutter, cut out biscuits.

Bake 15-20 minutes.

To dry out biscuits for longer shelf life, turn off the oven but don't remove the sheet of biscuits; keep them in there until the oven is completely cooled.

Makes approximately 12 medium-shaped dog biscuits.

Enjoy Pups! Jessica

Chapter 19

With both dogs now gone and Vinny feeling better but still not in remission, I decided it was time to concentrate on opening The Rolling Pin Cookie Café. I had the support of Vin and my family, all except one, yep, Mindi. She didn't think the cookie café was a good idea. In her opinion, she didn't think it would be successful, and it was more of a hobby than a business. What was different is it didn't matter if she supported me or not. I didn't *need* her approval. I didn't know why I wasted so many years seeking it. Why was it so important to me? I was going to do this my way, for me and no one else.

I made a business plan with the help of Jason and Vinny. I took out a small business loan and, with the help of a commercial real estate agent, started looking for the perfect place for The Rolling Pin Cookie Café. I found a storefront downtown where we lived. I hired contractors to lay the black and white tile flooring, upgrade my light fixtures and plumbing, and build counters. My family helped me with sweat equity, painting, and moving in the furniture. Two months later, I was ready to open The Rolling Pin Cookie Café. I had my vendors lined up, hired and trained my staff, and baked lots and lots of cookies, cupcakes, and dog treats

The day before the grand opening, I was so excited I could hardly sleep. I was up at 5 a.m. thinking about and preparing for tomorrow's events. The mayor and his staff would be there, giant scissors in hand for the ribbon-cutting ceremony and a

CHAPTER 19

photographer from the local paper. My team would be there with their Rolling Pin Cookie Café aprons on passing out free samples of cookies and shots of milk. I had the support of family, friends, all of whom would attend along with the locals. I served my community for years by word of mouth with my cookies, but this was the real deal. My other dream was finally coming true. As usual, making sure all the "I's" were dotted and "T's" were crossed, I had to make a last-minute stop to the craft store to pick up some odds and ends.

I arrived at the craft store and walked straight to the baking aisle to pick up a couple more cookie platters. I saw a little girl standing next to her mother. She was about four-years-old. She was wearing a pink sundress the length just below her knees with a ruffle on the bottom and white sandals. I noticed her toenails and fingernails were painted pink. She had long dark brown spiral curly hair that reached the middle of her back. She turned around and looked at me and sweetly said, "Hi," and gave me a little wave. I smiled and replied, "Hi, sweetie." She had big blue eyes and the sweetest angelic face. She was beautiful and perfect. She clung to her mommy's hand as they were leaving and looked back one more time and waved to me, and said, "Bye." I smiled and said, "Bye, sweetheart." She was exactly how I had imagined our little girl would look, a perfect combination of both Vinny and me. I took that as a sign from God, his gift to me, a final goodbye so that I could now focus on my other baby, The Rolling Pin Cookie Cafe. I checked out, gathered my things, and headed to the bakeshop.

* * *

It was finally the opening day! The coffee was brewing, hot water for tea, and the refrigerator was full of milk gallons. The armoire display shelves were packed with dry mixes and packaged baked cookies along with display knick-knacks, old-fashioned dishes, and glass milk bottles. Pictures of me and my Gram baking in the kitchen hung on the walls. The cookie display cases layered with an assortment of cookies, including chocolate chip, lemon crinkle sugar cookie, and the sweet and salty cookie, as well as cookie jars full of fresh baked goods. Let's not forget the small display case with canine goodies, Barkin' BBQ, peanut butter, and Lip Smackin' chicken dog biscuits, a fond memory of baking for my dogs. The edible raw cookie dough bar was fully stocked with sprinkles, gummy bears, and the like—best of all, the aroma of fresh-baked cookies lingering through the air. Happy thoughts of Gram flooded my mind and gave me a sense of peace.

Outside, I posed for pictures with the mayor by myself and with my staff and a final photo with my family. Finally, it was time to cut the ribbon. My stomach was doing summersaults. I had waited so long for this moment. The mayor and I placed our hands on the giant scissor and cut the ribbon together. Everyone cheered. Vin held the door open as everyone shuffled inside.

To the left against the wall were the white armoires with the packaged cookies, dry mixes, and knick-knacks. The edible raw cookie dough bar just next to them. In the middle were a few white tables and chairs. Just beyond the tables and chairs was the glass display case and counter with all the day's cookies, cupcakes, and other baked good choices. Located behind the counter was the kitchen where all the magic happened and a classroom where I taught cupcake and cookie decorating. The classroom also doubled as an area for children's cupcake and cookie decorating parties. To the right and towards the back was the book nook. Large bookshelves lined the walls with donated books, a sitting area with a large sofa and overstuffed chairs with end tables, and a coffee table in the middle. This area was a little quieter, where you could sit, relax, enjoy your cookie and beverage, and read a good book. Clubs could rent the book nook area and hold small meetings and enjoy cookies.

CHAPTER 19

My favorite memories were baking with my Gram. I loved spending time with her and baking, and the cookies were a bonus. I hoped that The Rolling Pin Cookie Cafe would help to create unforgettable memories for families. They would think of The Rolling Pin Cookie Café when celebrating something special.

The Rolling Pin Cookie Café had a steady stream of customers. I thought of the Field of Dreams quote, "If you build it, they will come," so I did. I built it, and they came in droves. I spent very little on marketing. My business was open just a few short months, and all my customers were word of mouth—orders to make cookie buffet tables for weddings, birthdays, and corporate events were rolling in. The holidays were coming, and I was already booked solid!

Today though was a quiet day. It was a Thursday and the first day back to school for the local children. I was sure to stay off social media today, as the first day of school, pictures were sure to flood my feed. I wanted to be one of those moms, taking photos on the first and last days of school. I wanted to be a room mom, too, making the holidays special for the children with my various goodies.

As I was filling the cookie jars with some fresh baked cookies, anticipating an after-school rush, I heard the familiar jingle of the bells I had hanging on my storefront door to alert me should I be in the back and a customer walks in. I looked up and saw a tall, thin woman with mousey brown hair, mid to late fifties, conservatively dressed. I greeted her, "Hi, I'm Jessica; welcome to The Rolling Pin Cookie Café. How may I help you today?" She smiled, one of those warm, pleasant smiles; it reminded me of my best friend Katherine, who was in heaven, oh how I missed her.

"Hi Jessica, I'm Darcy. What would you recommend?"

"Well, it depends on your taste. If you are a chocolate lover, I recommend our double chocolate chip cookie. It's a chocolate cookie with chocolate chips or our turtle cookie, a chocolate cookie topped with melted chocolate, caramel, and toasted pecans. A not-so-sweet cookie is our sugar shortbread cookie. A refreshing cookie is our lemon crinkle sugar cookie, and our most decadent cookie is our sweet and salty cookie. It's a chocolate chip cookie with pretzels, caramel bits, and sea salt."

"Oh, I'll try the sweet and salty cookie. It sounds delicious," Darcy said.

"Sure thing, coming right up. Would you like it warmed up?"

"Yes, please."

"Would you like a beverage? We have coffee, tea, milk, or hot cocoa."

"Tea, please."

"Coming right up, give me a minute to get the tea for you." I rang up her order we started some small talk.

"Slow day today?" she asked. "Usually, when I come in, it's super busy."

"Thank you for coming back," I replied. "Yes, it's usually busy, but it's the first day of school for the area children. I suspect it will be slow until about 2:30 or 3:00 when school lets out."

"Yes, I know," she said. "Do you have children?" she asked. There is was the question I had hoped to avoid all day.

"No," I replied. "I'm childless, not by choice." I saw her face light up a bit, yet sympathetic at the same time.

"Me too," she replied.

I handed her the warm, everything cookie and her tea. I touched her hand gently and said, "I'm sorry for your loss." At that moment, I wanted her to know; I understood and shared her pain.

"Thank you." A sense of relief came over her face, a silent understanding that we shared something. "I'm sorry for your loss, too," she said to me.

CHAPTER 19

"Thank you," I replied. Not wanting to elaborate on the conversation at this time, I changed the subject. "Feel free to make yourself comfortable on the sofa or one of our comfy oversized chairs and grab a book off the shelf and stay as long as you wish."

"Thank you. I brought a book," she patted her handbag, and I saw the book sticking out of the pocket.

"I'll leave you to it."

Darcy went and sat in one of the oversized chairs to enjoy her tea and fresh-baked goodies and read her book. I went back to filling the cookie jars.

Before she left, Darcy came up to me at the counter and gave me her business card, and said, "If you ever need anyone to talk about being childless, not by choice, I'm available."

"That would be nice; I think I would like that." I handed her my card and wrote my personal phone number on it.

I called Darcy the next day, and we made plans to meet for lunch the following Monday as The Rolling Pin Cookie Café was closed on Mondays. Darcy reminded me so much of Katherine; I felt she was heaven-sent. The more we talked, we found out how similar we were, yet our childless, not by choice journeys were different.

"May I ask you about your childless journey?" I asked.

"Sure," she said.

"I had been married but could not carry a child and suffered several miscarriages. My husband wanted biological children, and he divorced me. He married someone else, and they have four children together. I could never find a suitable partner after that or one who wanted to have children later in life. I tried the adoption route as a single woman but had no luck." This was the first time I had met someone who tried adoption and was unable to adopt because she was not chosen, just like Vin and myself.

Darcy and I met every Monday for lunch and became fast friends, and started hanging out all the time. We had so much in common. We both loved being creative. She was very good at jewelry making and photography, not to mention a fantastic cook. Vin and I had her over often. We prepared meals together and sat and talked or played games. We loved going to craft shows together when time permitted. Darcy and I were brainstorming one evening sitting on the patio after dinner, enjoying a glass of wine. The sun was going down, and Vin started a roaring fire in the fire pit for us. We talked about the lack of knowledge about being childless, not by choice, the lack of community, and how most of us suffer in silence.

"Darcy, there are so many women out there who have had miscarriages, but they never talk about it. Unfortunately, many women blame themselves saying things like, if I had just eaten healthier, exercised, stress less, worked less, if, if, if. I wish they knew- *It was not your fault. Stop blaming yourself.* Some women and men were never able to have biological children either due to health reasons or circumstances, but never talk about it. As childless, not by choice, women, and men, some people make us feel less than because we cannot have a biological child. Childless women are often said to be cat ladies, spinsters, or old hag. Men are often thought of as weak, not manly, weird, or odd not only by society but by family and friends too."

That's when I had my ah-ha moment.

"Hey Darcy, what if we start a private online community and blog for childless men and women?"

"I think that's a great idea, Jess!"

We decided then and there to start this online community to embrace others like us. After much discussion and writing every thought in a brainstorming session, we honed what we wanted this online community's goals to be. We called it: We Are Childless Not By Choice – Healing Through The Hurt Together. Our goal was to help childless women and men through the grieving process of losing a baby or not being able to have children either for medical reasons or circumstances.

CHAPTER 19

Darcy and I put our heads together and conceptualized topics we wanted to discuss in our blog. They included; what to say and how to react when someone says something inappropriate about being childless. Another blog idea was how to navigate holidays and other family gatherings and the crucial topics, aging childless and disenfranchised grief. We were on fire! Our community would be able to openly and freely discuss being childless, not by choice, with no judgment. We would be able to vent about something someone said or did to trigger us that day and have a community of people who understood. We will help those who are grieving, angry, or depressed. We will help our community to find another dream and fulfill what God intended for us.

Over the next couple of months, we started building our website, writing our blog, and getting onto social media platforms. Our first blog post was born.

* * *

Our first blog post:
Didn't your mom ever tell you, if you can't say something nice, don't say anything at all?
We've all been there, at a family or work event, and someone says something inappropriate to us about being childless, not by choice. We are shocked that someone could say something so insensitive and think nothing of it. We try to keep our composure. Sometimes we have to excuse ourselves from these toxic people as not to become angry and cause a scene or sneak away to the bathroom to compose ourselves to prevent a complete and utter meltdown. Without even knowing it, they have hurt us and made us feel like we are defective in some way. **We are not.** We cannot possibly prepare for every insensitive remark someone says to us, but we can choose how to react. We can tell them it's an inappropriate thing to say or it's private, and none of your business or simply walk away.

Don't let what someone says have power over you. Below is a brief list of insensitive, unsolicited comments zinged at us, the writers of this blog, over the years. These comments trivialize the loss of a child and the want to have a child. Take a minute to read them over and think of how you would respond. Then think about how you might react. We would love for you to leave a comment below in the comment section and let us know how you might respond. Please abide by our blog rules and guidelines, no profanity, and if replying to someone else's comment, please be courteous.

- You must not have really wanted children, or you would have had them.
- If you stop trying, you will get pregnant.
- God has another plan for you.
- Maybe God knew you wouldn't make a good parent.
- Do you want to throw me a baby shower?
- If you adopt, would we still have a shower for you?
- I'm thinking about having an abortion.
- I had four kids; as soon as I had them, I realized I didn't want to be a mother.
- You can be a mother/father to your friend's kids
- Just adopt!
- Whose fault is it that you can't have children? Yours or your husband's?
- You're so lucky not to have kids.
- You must have a lot of money.
- You're lucky your husband didn't divorce you.
- When are you going to have kids?

CHAPTER 19

- Are you pregnant yet?
- I'm only inviting other parents to my child's birthday party.
- You're lucky; you get to sleep in, travel and shop.
- You don't know what love is until you have a child.
- Children make your life complete.
- You become less selfish after you have children.
- Who is going to take care of you when you are old?
- Don't you feel that something is missing in your life?
- Can you take my holiday shift? You don't have kids.
- After a miscarriage, well, at least you know you can get pregnant.
- Get over it; you didn't know that baby anyway.
- You're young; you can try again.
- How long are you going to grieve for a child you never knew?

* * *

Our We Are Childless Not By Choice blog and the private online community began to grow. We found a small group of local people who were reading and commenting on our blog. We decided to start having support group meetings in person, two times a month at The Rolling Pin Cookie Café, after hours in the book nook area. I was both excited and nervous. I was eager to finally meet more men and women who shared my story but uneasy about the aspect of opening wounds that were on the mend but not yet fully healed.

MY SECRET GRIEF

Sweet & Salty Cookies

Ingredients:

1 cup butter*
1-1/2 teaspoons vanilla extract
1-1/2 cups brown sugar
1-1/2 cup granulated sugar
2 large eggs
2-1/2 cups all-purpose flour
2-1/2 teaspoons baking powder
1/2 teaspoon sea salt plus more for sprinkling
3/4 cup broken pretzels, plus more for top
1-1/2 cups caramel bits (Kraft brand)
3/4 cup semisweet chocolate chips

Directions:

- Line cookie sheet with parchment paper. Preheat oven to 350 degrees.

- *Brown the butter- in saucepan melt butter over medium heat, whisking as it melts, foams and bubbles. Little brown bits will form, and butter will turn amber. Immediately pour into a heatproof bowl making sure to get all the brown bits.

- Using a mixer, beat the vanilla and sugars into the butter until the color lightens.

- Beat in eggs.

- Add the baking powder, 1/2 teaspoon of salt, and one-third of the flour. Mix slowly, add another third, mix, and add the last of the four until combined.

- Stir in the pretzels, caramel bits, and chocolate chips.

- Scoop out onto prepared cookie sheet, leaving space between cookies. Add more broken pretzels, caramel

CHAPTER 19

bits, and chocolate chips to the tops of the cookie dough balls. Sprinkle with sea salt.

- Bake 10-13 minutes, depending on the size of cookies, until golden around the edges.
- Cool completely.
- Best if served warm.

Enjoy! Jessica

Chapter 20

Our blog had been online for a few months now, and our local members wanted to meet in person. Tonight after The Rolling Pin Cookie Café closed, our We Are Childless Not By Choice local community would gather in the book nook area. For the first time, I was not nervous about meeting new people. Although I had not met them in person, I felt I already knew them from the painful stories of their lives they had shared online in our private group.

It was 7 p.m. I had just finished setting up the cookies and beverages in the book nook area. Darcy was at the front of the bakery by the door, waiting to greet our members as they arrived. Everyone arrived promptly. Darcy locked the door behind them, flipped the door sign to closed, and walked them back to the book nook area. Darcy and I stood in front of our small group, there were six of us total, and we introduced ourselves. "Hello, everyone. Welcome to our first in-person gathering of the We Are Childless, Not By Choice community. I'm Jessica, and this is Darcy. We are so happy to have you here. Please help yourself to cookies and a beverage and make yourself comfortable on the couch or in one of our overstuffed chairs, and we will start in a few minutes." Everyone shuffled over to the cookie buffet area I had set up and helped themselves to the variety of goodies that I had laid out and promptly found a comfortable spot to sit. We had both men and women. Several of the members looked to be around my age of fifty or slightly older, with two women looking to be in their forties.

I started the meeting. "I want to thank you all for being here. I'm very excited to meet our local community members. I want to reiterate we will follow the same rules here at our in-person meeting as we do in our online community. This is a safe space to talk about our feelings or uncomfortable situations we have encountered being childless, not by choice. I ask that you do not use profanity and be respectful when someone else is speaking. If a family member or friend is pregnant, trying to get pregnant, or just gave birth to a baby, please do not talk about it. Do not bring in pictures or share the news in our online group. We never know what may trigger someone. Lastly, this is not a dating group. This is a group for men and women who are childless, not by choice and are no longer pursuing parenthood. That said, let's go around the room and introduce ourselves and tell us a little bit about yourself and your childless, not by choice journey. We'll keep it to five minutes or less per person for today, and in future meetings, we can dive into situations a little more in-depth. Let's start here with this gentleman to my left."

The tall thin clean-cut professional-looking man, with white hair, spoke first. "Hi everyone, my name is Jim. I married a woman who never wanted children. I knew this going into the marriage. I thought she would change her mind over time, but she didn't. I am a business consultant and focused on work, filling my time and the void of not having children. As a result of focusing solely on my career, my marriage ended. I realized that life was passing me by, and I wasn't enjoying it. I decided to start my own consulting business, and I now work where and when I want. I get to choose the projects I want to work on, and it has proven to be a very successful business. I always thought I would be a dad someday, but I guess that was not in the cards for me. I never remarried. I don't know anyone who is childless like me in my family and friends, so I was happy to find this online group. It's a great chance to talk to people and work through some of my issues. Oh, one last thing, I have a passion for photography as a hobby. Thanks for listening."

Everyone clapped. "Thank you for sharing, Jim," I said. I thought this was a good start, and I was feeling grateful for our little group.

Next up was a woman who looked to be in her forties. She had medium-length straight blond hair with an athletic build. "Hello, I'm Sally. I was diagnosed with cancer in my mid-twenties, and as a result, I cannot have children. I'm married to my wonderful husband for 25 years, and I'm a proud canine mom. I'm also an elementary school teacher, and I believe that was God's plan for me. I feel I'm here where I belong with all of you to help me through some tough times, particularly events involving my family. I feel like the black sheep of the family. My husband and I recently found out my siblings have been going on vacations together with their children for years. My husband and I were not invited. It makes me wonder how else we have been excluded. I am happy I found this group and hope I can find answers on how to navigate through family situations like these. Thanks." Again, everyone clapped.

"Welcome, Sally, we are happy you are here, and we will absolutely help you in any way we can," Darcy said.

Next, our young-ish early forties woman spoke. She was the cute nerdy type with long brown hair, and she wore black-rimmed glasses. She was petite and fair-skinned. "Hi, I'm April." She gave a little wave to the group. "I've always been quiet and shy. I have a small group of friends, all married with children. I have a niece and a nephew that I enjoy spending time with, and I adore them. I'm a research assistant at a law firm. Mostly, I enjoy being home with my cat, reading a good book. I guess you could say I'm a homebody. The man I thought was the love of my life cheated on me and, and the

CHAPTER 20

girl ended up pregnant, and he married her. Since then, I've never dated anyone long enough even to consider marriage. Before I knew it, my optimal childbearing years were over. My family and friends make remarks about my childless status. I was researching the topic, how to handle family comments when you are single, and I came across your website and blog and decided to join. I'm active in the online community and feel all of you really get me. I'm happy to be here." Everyone clapped again.

"Welcome, April. We are so happy you found us online. It's nice to put a face with those who are active in our community," I said.

"Well, I guess I'm next." A deep masculine voice said. He was bald, with a reddish-brown beard and mustache and a little on the chunky side, late fifties, maybe early sixties, but that was a guess. My first impression of him was that of a happy-go-lucky, out-going guy. He was very personable with everyone while he was getting his cookies. "Hello everyone, my name is Sam. I'm a high school history teacher here locally. I fell in love with my high school sweetheart at the age of sixteen. We had our entire life planned out. We were going to get married after we graduated from college and start a family. We went to the same college and got engaged after we graduated. We were married a year later. After about three years of marriage, we decided it was time to start a family. We tried for years to become pregnant and finally sought out an infertility specialist and found it was me with the problem. We tried the IVF treatments, and they didn't work and were very expensive. Adoption was a long wait and too costly. We decided to foster children. We fostered children for a few years, but it broke our hearts every time we had to send a child back to their biological parent. Emotionally, we couldn't take it anymore and stopped. Unfortunately, a couple of years ago, my wife died of cancer. I've been working with a therapist to help me with the grieving process of losing my wife, and

I realized that I was also grieving not having children. I was looking online for a group of people who were grieving the loss of a child they never had. A dream never realized just like mine, and I found We Are Childless Not By Choice. This community has brought me a lot of peace, and I'm just hoping to pay it forward. God bless each and every one of you. Thank you." Lots of clapping for Sam. A sense of relief washed over his face.

"Thank you, Sam," Darcy said. "This is precisely why we started this online group to help each other through difficult times. We understand that losing our dream of having a child needs to be grieved, just like any other loss."

"I guess I'm next," Darcy said. "Hello everyone, my name is Darcy. I am an accountant and co-founder of the We are Childless Not By Choice blog and online community. I had been married but could not carry a child and suffered several miscarriages. We tried IVF treatments, and those failed too. My husband wanted biological children and did not want to adopt, and after fifteen years of marriage, he divorced me. He married someone else, and they have four children together. I could never find a suitable partner after that or one who wanted to have children later in life. I tried the adoption route as a single woman but had no luck. I then met Jessica. I believe God put me in Jessica's path. As we got to know each other and talked a lot about our childless journeys, although different, in the end, we were both grieving the loss of a child we never had. We didn't want others to suffer the way we had been, and the We Are Childless Not By Choice blog and online community was born. We hope to open communication lines between our family, friends, and society to let them know that their inappropriate comments cut us like a knife and leave invisible scars. Being childless not by choice is an awkward subject because most people don't understand it. They don't understand how we can grieve for a baby we never had. We put on a mask and pretend everything is okay. We

CHAPTER 20

avoid certain situations. We grieve in silence. But together, in this little group of ours, it's okay to vent your frustrations. It's okay to talk about why an inappropriate comment someone made sent you into an uncontrollable crying fit. It's okay to be angry. Together all of us here tonight make up a unique family where we love each other, show compassion for each other, and support each other." Loud applause for Darcy.

"Well, how do I follow that?" Chuckles from the group. "Hello, my name is Jessica. As you know, I'm the owner of The Rolling Pin Cookie Café and co-founder of We Are Childless Not By Choice. My story is a little like Sam's. I met the love of my life, and we were married and ready to start a family. It took years and years; we tried many medical procedures, medications, and several doctors. It turns out; I was perfectly healthy. It was my husband, Vinny, who was not."

"We went through IVF treatments and had one viable egg for implantation. I was thrilled to see the ultrasound where my baby girl was implanted into my uterus. It all came to a crashing end one day when I got the phone call from the nurse that said the implantation did not take. Sadly, that ultrasound would be the one and only picture I would ever see of my baby girl." A couple of members of the group nodded their heads; they understood.

"I kept my emotions hidden from my family and friends as best I could and eventually stopped seeing family and friends altogether. I went into a deep depression coupled with anxiety and anger, which lasted years. I later discovered this is called disenfranchised grief." Again, more silent head nodding from the group and a couple of un-huh's. "During this time, we also tried adoption, but we were never chosen. Many of us in this room share similar stories," my hand gestured towards Darcy and Sam. It took me years to understand that my experience and loss were for a higher purpose. I was mad at God for a long, long time. I couldn't comprehend how he could let people abuse children or, worse, allow parents to murder their children. Here I am wanting children but could not have them, nor could I adopt them."

"I knew in my heart I would be a great mom, and Vinny would be a great dad; there was no doubt in my mind. Every single day, and I know many of you have dealt with this in your lives; you're feeling good, you've accepted your childless status. You've done all you could to try and have a biological baby. You've attempted to adopt or whatever your journey was to try and become a parent. You're feeling okay this particular day, and you're like, *okay, I'm feeling a little bit better. I think I can get through the day,* and then WHAM! It happens; someone says some insensitive remark and sends you spiraling back down into your hole of depression." Heads of our group members nodded in agreement, along with some voices.

"You think to yourself, why hasn't God blessed me with a child? It's not fair; I would have been a great parent. There are many days that I wished I was in heaven with my babies. Somehow, I was exactly the opposite of where I thought I would be in my life. I could not grasp what happened. I still don't understand. I will never know why I wasn't blessed with a child. Most days, I wanted to hide under the blankets and never come out. I felt foolish for dreaming about my baby shower or picking out names and clothes for my baby or decorating her nursery." April dabbed tears from her eyes with a tissue. "I had such high hopes, and I never thought that I wouldn't be a parent. The thought never crossed my mind, but here it was, staring me in the face. My more than twenty-year journey to becoming a mother was over. I had to find the meaning in all of this. With the help of my husband, therapist, and my friend Darcy, I did."

"Showing grief doesn't have any rules or instructions. There is no normal, and it takes as long as it takes; everyone is different. There will always be a hole in my heart that will never be filled, no matter how much I try. I try to keep myself busy as best as possible, but there are still days when I

CHAPTER 20

feel defeated. I can't even go to the park and enjoy it because someone asked which child is yours and I have to reply, I don't have one. Then they look at me like I'm some kind of a creeper weirdo because I'm hanging out at the park where kids are playing. All I wanted to do was go there to read a book, enjoy the fresh air and nature, and relieve some stress. It's the little things in life that we take for granted, and we all need to be a bit more mindful of what somebody else may be going through. You never know what someone is going through or has gone through. All we can do is be better people, be sensitive to others' feelings, and help those who need help."

"I guess the way I was able to contribute to my family and friends and show them that I love them is through my baking and crafting. I bake from scratch. I don't skimp on the quality. I always use the best, freshest ingredients and pour my whole heart into it. This is my way of relieving depression, stress, and anxiety. I didn't know I was doing it. I was just trying to fill a void, an emptiness in my heart that never went away and never will go away. It was my way to show my love for my family and friends and to express myself. It is my creative outlet, and I hope my family and friends get it. I took the time to bake this for you, or I made this gift for you because I love you. That's my story. Thanks for listening." More clapping from the group.

We all sat and talked a little longer and ate cookies until the meeting ended at 8 p.m. After everyone left, I turned to Darcy, "I would say our evening was a success!" She agreed, and we hugged.

As the weeks went by, we talked to our community online, and in person, something amazing started happening. Our little group started healing together. We helped each other; we held each other up when we needed to. We started socializing outside of the group as well. I finally found my group of people who truly understood what I was going through. They understood when an off-handed comment out in our daily life threw one of us into a crying fit, where we wanted to stay locked in our house for days. With the support of this new family, there was no judgment, and everyone was healing together.

Our little group was thriving, and I decided to open up The Rolling Pin Cookie Café to other area groups and organizations. On different afternoons of the week, small local groups rented out the book nook area of the café. We had the Girl Scouts, Boy Scouts, a bible study group, and a women's book club.

I had never thought that talking through my grief and sharing my story would benefit others. Growing up, I was taught we don't talk about our feelings. We are somehow weak or crazy if we want to speak to a psychiatrist. God had put me through this experience, healed me, and showed me that I could help someone else by sharing my story. Men, women, and couples need to share their grief to heal and move on. We will always wonder what our child or children would look like, who they would have become, their passions, strengths, and weaknesses, the friends they would have, and the family they would have started.

The grief of losing a child will never go away. The pain may lessen, but it will never truly be gone. We never had the pleasure of meeting our child or children. They will hold a special place in our hearts forever until we are reunited in eternity.

Gram's Bohemian Apple Strudel

Dough Ingredients:

2 cups flour
2 eggs
1/2 cup lukewarm water
1 tablespoon white vinegar
2 tablespoons lard
Pinch of salt

Dough Directions:

Mix all ingredients well until dough is not sticky and does not stick to hands. Shape into a mound and cover with a heated bowl and let rest for about 15 minutes to half an hour. If the bowl cools, replace the bowl with another heated bowl. The dough must be warm when ready to stretch. With hands floured, on a lightly floured clean towel, begin to stretch the dough pulling from the center with fingers; take care not to tear the dough. Continue to stretch until the dough is paper-thin (you should be able to read the recipe through the dough) and rectangular in shape.

Filling:

2-1/2 pounds apples, Jonathan or Roman Beauty, peeled and sliced
1 cup sugar
Rind from 1 lemon
1 tablespoon cinnamon
1/2 cup golden raisins (soaked in rum, brandy, apple juice, or lukewarm water until plump)
1 cup breadcrumbs
4-6 oz melted butter

Directions:

Melt half of the butter in a sauté pan and add breadcrumbs. Stir until all the butter is absorbed and breadcrumbs are no longer dry, set aside. In a separate bowl, mix cinnamon and sugar and set aside.

In a large bowl, combined peeled and sliced apples, golden raisins, lemon rind, cinnamon, and sugar mixture and mix well.

Sprinkle stretched dough with the buttered breadcrumbs, top with apple mixture, spreading out evenly and thinly, about an inch and a half from the sides, drizzle with more melted butter.

Roll up jelly-roll style on the short end and transfer to a non-stick baking sheet with the help of the towel. The dough should be seam side down, and corners tucked in. Remove towel. Brush strudel with melted butter and bake 1/2 hour at 374 degrees until golden brown. Just before serving, sprinkle with powdered sugar if desired.

Enjoy! Jessica

About the Author

Jayme Lynn lives in the Western Suburbs of Chicago with her husband and two rescued Italian Greyhounds. She enjoys writing, scrapbooking, making handmade cards, favors, and baking, which serves as a creative outlet for her grief. These are just a few ways she shows her love for family and friends. She is passionate about helping other childless not by choice women and men work through their grief to find purpose and joy in their life.

Connect with Jayme Lynn at www.jaymelynn.com.

www.ingramcontent.com/pod-product-compliance
Lightning Source LLC
LaVergne TN
LVHW011829060526
838200LV00053B/3950